"You know they don't really expect you to stay forever," he said in a low voice, which necessitated him walking close enough so he could smell her.

She smelled mostly like sunscreen and a bug spray designed to smell better than it actually worked.

"In Stonefield time, six months *is* forever."

He laughed. "Come on. We're not that bad."

When she tilted her head and put her hands on her hips, he braced himself for a verbal blast. But she just glared at him for a few seconds before she spoke in a voice as low as his. "No, some of the people here aren't that bad."

Grinning, he nudged her shoulder with his. "How about me? How bad am I?"

It wasn't until the words had left his mouth that he realized that was a question that could be taken in a couple of ways. He hadn't intended any innuendo at all, but she might read some into the question. And when she glanced sideways at him, her eyebrow arched, he held his breath, but she shook her head.

"You've been a pain in the ass since we were kids," she said, amusement in her voice. "But I guess you're not *that* bad."

Dear Reader,

Her Hometown Man is the first book in a new series that brings together many things dear to my heart. Over the course of my career, I've written a lot about brothers and brotherhood because I love that dynamic. I have four sisters, though, and I love the bonds that we share. I also love small towns and the local watering holes that become gathering places for the community—to quote a favorite old television show, the kind of place where everybody knows your name.

In the Sutton's Place series, three sisters come together to help their mother achieve their father's dream of opening just such a place. Gwen Sutton, the oldest sister, returns to her hometown thinking she can hide the lifelong crush she's had on the man who lives across the street, but she's very wrong. And the more time Case Danforth and his adorable dog (another thing I love) spend on *her* side of the street, the harder it gets.

You can find out what I'm up to and keep up with book news on my website, www.shannonstacey.com, where you'll find the latest information, as well as a link to sign up for my newsletter. And you can also reach me by emailing shannon@shannonstacey.com or look me up on Facebook at Facebook.com/shannonstacey.authorpage.

I hope you enjoy Gwen and Case's story, and welcome to Sutton's Place!

Shannon

Her Hometown Man

SHANNON STACEY

Recycling programs for this product may not exist in your area.

ISBN-13: 978-1-335-40828-0

Her Hometown Man

Harlequin Enterprises ULC
22 Adelaide St. West, 41st Floor
Toronto, Ontario M5H 4E3, Canada
www.Harlequin.com

Printed in U.S.A.

A *New York Times* and *USA TODAY* bestselling author of over forty romances, **Shannon Stacey** grew up military and lived many places before landing in a small New Hampshire town where she has resided with her husband and two sons for over twenty years. Her favorite activities are reading and writing with her dogs at her side. She also loves coffee, Boston sports and watching too much TV. You can learn more about her books at www.shannonstacey.com.

Visit the Author Profile page
at Harlequin.com for more titles.

For my four younger sisters. You're amazing and fierce and magic in your own unique ways, and I love you all. Being your big sister is one of the greatest joys in my life, and not just because being the oldest means never having to sit in the back seat.

Chapter One

Rumor has it Stonefield's own Gwen Sutton is back in town. She relocated to Vermont following the huge success of A Quaking of Aspens *(which may or may not have been based on Stonefield, and we certainly all have opinions about that) but according to one informed reader, she might be staying here in New Hampshire for a while.*

—Stonefield Gazette *Facebook Page*

"Well, look at that. Gwen Sutton's home again."

Case Danforth heard his cousin's statement and looked up from the small laptop he had propped on his knees. They co-owned the tree service left to them by their fathers, and every Saturday night they sat on Case's front porch and didn't allow themselves to have a beer or go out until the paperwork was completed. It was the only way the administrative tasks ever got done.

But the goings-on at the Sutton house across the street were a lot more interesting than reviewing the increases in their insurance costs, so he watched as the small silver sedan with Vermont plates parked between two SUVs. He knew she'd turned the ignition off because the lights eventually went dark, but the door didn't open. Apparently Gwen was just going to sit in her car for a while.

"This might not bode well for you, Lane," he said, closing the laptop and setting it on the table next to him. It was going to be a few minutes before they got back to the paperwork.

His cousin shook his head. "No, it doesn't. If Gwen's home, Mallory probably asked her to come, which means there's a problem. And a problem for the Sutton family could be bad for me."

Mallory was the middle Sutton sister, and the only one who'd stayed in Stonefield. Gwen, who was the oldest, had been the first to move away. Then Evie had gone, leaving Mallory to hold down the fort, so to speak.

Boomer snuffled in his sleep and nudged Case's leg, so he reached down and scratched the top of the dog's head. Boomer—so named because they'd returned from lunch one day to find him asleep under the boom truck—had decided immediately that Case was his person. When all efforts to identify the dog had failed, Case had surrendered to the inevitable. He was pretty sure Boomer was a mix of German shepherd and black Lab, and the former's intelligence when it came to training mixed with the latter's basic predisposition to loving the outdoors and being content to sleep in or under a truck made him the perfect companion for Case. And for Lane, too, since they were together so often. But Case was definitely his person.

"Maybe they're doing some kind of memorial for their dad," he suggested to Lane, trying to be optimistic. Maybe Gwen coming home had nothing to do with the business Lane had started with David Sutton.

"I probably would have heard something about a memorial in the works," his cousin said, and he wasn't wrong.

When Lane and David Sutton had decided to invest everything they had into finally opening the brewery they'd been talking about for many years, Case had had some reservations, but he kept most of them to himself. And things had gone well for a while. Lane was the brewer and, while it took him away from the tree service more than Case would have liked, his cousin was happy so they made it work. David loved the brewing, too, but he was also the idea man, owned the carriage house they were converting into a tavern and would coordinate everything to do with the public.

Nobody had seen the heart attack coming. David's passing had left them all reeling, but with so much on the line financially for Lane, he'd had to keep pushing toward the goal. Ellen, David's widow, had told Case she was determined to make the brewery a success in honor of her husband's dream, with Mallory's help. But Gwen coming home probably meant Mallory was desperate for help.

"I guess if there's something big going on, Evie will show up anytime," Lane said, and the wooden rocker creaked as he shifted his weight.

She'd been another of Case's reservations about the whole endeavor. His cousin and Evie Sutton had been married for all of a year after Lane returned from college, and going into business with his former father-in-law was a tie with his ex-wife Case wasn't sure Lane needed. Lane had brushed it off as not a big deal, but that was easy to say when the woman in question was rarely seen in Stonefield.

"How are you going to handle that?" Case asked.

"Same as I handle every other day of my life. Cut some trees. Brew some beer. Drink some beer. Sleep and repeat." He chuckled, but it sounded a little forced. "Evie and I are very, very ancient history."

He'd let Lane keep telling himself that for now. Case had a theory that the primary reason his cousin hadn't settled down over the years since his divorce was that Lane's brain might think his feelings for Evie were ancient history, but his heart didn't.

Across the street, the car door opened and Case watched Gwen slowly climb out of the driver's seat. She was wearing a light cardigan over leggings, with her long blond hair piled in a messy knot on her head. He wasn't close enough to see her expression, but he'd grown up with the Sutton sisters and he knew she'd look tense. Being the most introverted and serious of them, she often looked closed off. Resting bitch face, he thought it was called.

But Case also knew she had a smile that lit up her face. And when she really let herself go and laughed, everybody in the room had to laugh with her. Her joy was infectious, but she usually kept it buttoned up. Especially when she was in Stonefield.

When she popped the trunk, Case's eyebrow shot up. "She brought a lot of luggage."

"What do you think the chances are she just decided to come home and it has nothing to do with the brewery?"

"It's possible. I mean, she really doesn't like it here, but with her dad gone, maybe she wants to be back here with her mom." But that didn't feel right to him. They all knew Gwen was happy in Vermont, and that she and her mother remained close despite the distance.

Lane sighed and then pushed himself to his feet. "It's time for a beer."

Boomer lifted his head, probably to see if Lane

was going to do something interesting like throw a stick or fry up a pan of bacon, but he'd only had nine or ten naps that day and was exhausted. He was snoring again before Lane reached the door.

"We're not done with our work," Case protested, waving his hand at the laptop. But he could see the tension in his cousin's face. "Breakfast meeting tomorrow?"

"Sounds good." Lane disappeared into the house and came back with a beer for each of them. They were from a brewery in the southern part of the state they'd visited last weekend—Case didn't mind the research trips at all—and they sipped in silence for a few minutes.

"Ellen and Mal keep telling me everything's okay. They've shown me plans and projections and stuff. But the execution…it's hard to tell. I think it's going okay, but we need to be *more* than okay at this point. And trying to balance being pushy with respecting the fact that the woman lost her husband six months ago is hard." He sighed and shook his head. "It's all well and good to say it's strictly business, but I've known Ellen my whole life. She's one of my mom's best friends. Hell, she was my mother-in-law."

"After we finished the paperwork, I was going to tell you Ellen caught me on my way in tonight. She asked if I could come over and look at a few things in the carriage house."

"Why didn't she ask me?"

Case shrugged. "I don't know. But she knows

what the stakes are for you, so maybe she's feeling some pressure to keep up an appearance everything's good. I've been helping out around the property since David died, so maybe it's easier for her to ask me for help."

"Just keep me in the loop, please."

"You know I will."

When an ancient Jeep Wrangler pulled into the Sutton driveway and parked half on the grass next to one of the SUVs, Case leaned forward in his rocker. Unlike her oldest sister, Evie Sutton wasted no time getting out and, after opening the back door, she started piling totes and a few boxes on the ground.

The youngest sister also had blond hair—all three of them did, like their mother—but hers was shorter than Gwen's, and a lighter shade. Mallory's color was in-between, and her hair was shoulder-length and wavier than Gwen's. Despite the differences, there was never any doubt the three women were sisters.

"She's got a lot of stuff, too," Case said, not that he needed to. His cousin's gaze was locked onto his ex-wife. "Maybe we should go over there and offer to help carry stuff in."

As Gwen walked over to Evie and the two sisters exchanged what could only be described as a perfunctory hug, Lane chuckled. "Nope. I want no part of whatever's going on over there tonight."

Case sat back in his rocking chair and took a sip of his beer. "Things are definitely about to get interesting."

* * *

Gwen would have happily sat in her car for a while more—hours, even—rather than go inside, but Evie had texted them all to say she'd stopped at the market and would be home in a few minutes.

Home.

Back in her small, suffocating hometown in the middle of New Hampshire. She hadn't expected to be back until December. She'd begged off last Christmas—claiming deadlines as she always did—doing a FaceTime chat with the family instead. She'd had to come home anyway, in the middle of January for her dad's funeral. Missing out on sharing his love for the holidays and getting one last hug would haunt her forever.

Without being told, she'd known she'd have to be home for the family's first Christmas without Dad. But here she was, at the halfway point of the year, with the bare minimum of things she'd need for the summer. She was hoping not to be in Stonefield for that long, but Mal had been sketchy on the details when she called.

Gwen had been munching on a carrot stick—which absolutely was *not* a satisfying replacement for her beloved Doritos, regardless of crunch and color—and staring at a whiteboard covered in plot points scrawled on sticky notes when the phone rang. She'd answered it and heard Mal's voice.

"You need to come home."

"The hell I do," Gwen had responded.

"Gwen." Her sister had managed to inject an entire paragraph's worth of exasperation into that one word.

"Mallory."

When the answering silence had stretched on, Gwen had resigned herself to making another trip home. As much as the good people of Stonefield got on her last nerve and no matter how behind she was on her book, if her family really needed her, she wouldn't say no.

So now here she was, back in the house she'd grown up in with her mom and her sisters. It would feel like she'd stepped through a time warp, if not for the constant awareness that her father was no longer with them.

Though the house had a huge formal dining room thanks to its pre-Suttons life as an inn, they were seated around the small kitchen table, as always. The kitchen was the heart of Ellen's home and they'd always taken their meals there. For as long as Gwen could remember, the massive cherry dining room table was for doing jigsaw puzzles, eating Thanksgiving dinner and wrapping Christmas presents.

Mallory's two boys—ten-year-old Jack and Eli, who was eight—had been granted video game time in the family room after greeting their aunts, and as her mom made them all tea because she believed tea was always a cure for what ailed a person, Gwen listened to the sounds of engines racing and juvenile trash talk.

And she stared at the empty chair at the head of the table—her dad's chair. Her mom's favorite summer cardigan was slung over the back, and Gwen wasn't sure if it was simply where Ellen had mindlessly tossed it, or if she'd put it there to keep people from sitting in the spot her husband had occupied for over thirty years.

"it's so good to have all my girls home again," her mom said, as she pulled out the chair to the right of the empty one—where she'd not only been next to her husband, but closest to the stove—with a tea of her own. Her smile was warm but quivering slightly. "I'm sorry to be such a bother, though."

It was Mal, of course, who reached over and covered their mother's hand with her own. Mal was the peacemaker—the one who interceded and arbitrated and soothed. Maybe it was because she was the middle child, though she didn't really bridge the gap between the eldest and youngest. At thirty-five, Mal was only a year younger than Gwen. But there had been seven years between Mal and a surprise Evie and even at twenty-eight, their youngest sister seemed irresponsible and immature to Gwen. Evie thought Gwen was uptight and controlling. Mal had always had her work cut out for her when it came to keeping the peace between them.

"You know we're always here when you need us, Mom," Gwen said. And then she turned her gaze to Mallory. "You said you'd explain everything when we got here. Well…we're here."

What followed was Mallory recapping the last six months of handling their father's estate, while Ellen wrapped her hands around her warm mug and held it so tightly, Gwen was afraid it might crack. The bottom line was that David Sutton had put everything they had into turning the carriage house into a brewery and if it wasn't a success, their mom could end up with nothing.

Gwen swallowed the questions that popped into her head first—how could her father have been so irresponsible and how could her mother have let him—and focused on the immediate issue. "What, exactly, is it you expect us to do about the brewery?"

"Help. I expect you to help."

"I hate to break it to you, Mal, but I don't know a damn thing about brewing beer."

"The brewer is handling the brewing, of course."

"Okay." Gwen waited, but her sister didn't offer any more information. "If the brewer is handling the brewing, then the brewing is handled. Problem solved and, I repeat, what do you expect me to do?"

"There's a lot more to running the business than the actual making of the beer. We have to finish renovating the space and make sure we stick to the business plan and plan a menu and go through a metric ton of checklists."

"And hire staff," Evie added.

When Mal shrugged and made a *well* sound, Gwen got it. And she didn't like it. "You expect us to be free labor, don't you? Bartender? Server?"

"Dibs on *not* being the dishwasher." Evie practically shouted in her rush to get the words out.

"If everybody pitches in, we can do this," Mallory said.

"I have a job," Gwen reminded her. "One that I actually get paid for."

"We can try to keep you at half days so you can still write. Maybe they can give you a little more time to write your book—an extension or whatever?"

Gwen's stomach knotted at the idea of asking for another deadline extension. The writing hadn't been going well *before* their father died, and it certainly hadn't gotten any easier since. "It's not that simple, Mal."

"I don't know if we can do it without you," her sister said somberly.

Ellen sighed and blinked back unshed tears. "The last thing I want is to ask you girls to put your lives on hold, but the thrift shop can't support this house, me, Mallory and the boys, *and* the loans your father took out. If the brewery doesn't succeed, I'll lose everything."

Gwen's heart ached at the hopelessness in her mom's voice, and she focused on her mom's hand in Mal's because the pain in her eyes was too much. It wasn't until she saw her sister's hand trembling that it hit her that Mallory would lose everything, too. She'd moved home with her sons after her marriage fell apart, and she'd started working at the thrift shop with their mother. It was an arrangement that had worked well for everybody, but her life was so intertwined with her parents' that she had no safety net of her own.

There was absolutely no way Gwen could get back in her car and drive away, leaving them to figure it out while she tried to help and advise from a distance. "How much debt are we talking about?"

Her mother quoted a number that instantly made Gwen's stomach hurt. "Mom. How…?"

She let the questions die away. *How could Dad do that to you? How could you let him do that?* Saying the words would only hurt, not help.

"Gwen, do you…?" Mallory looked down at the table and shook her head, letting the question fade away.

She didn't need to finish it, though. Gwen knew that the perception of a bestselling author's income and the reality were not one and the same. "I can maybe help a little, but I can't put a dent in that. Most of the stuff people see—the book clubs and the movie and all that—was baked into my first contract and debut authors don't have a lot of negotiating power. And I signed the contract for the second and third book before *A Quaking of Aspens* broke out, and my agent gets his cut and don't even get me started on taxes. I got more for my current book but it's not done. So, like I said, I can help a little, but not enough to make this problem go away."

Honestly, the best thing she could do was go home

and finish the book and get the rest of her advance, but even that wouldn't be enough.

"I wouldn't want to take your money, anyway," Ellen said, but Gwen and Mallory locked gazes and she knew if she had it to give, they would take it.

"How is the business partner handling things?" Gwen asked after an awkward silence, and the look that passed between her mom and Mallory filled her with dread.

"He stands to lose his investment, too," Mal answered. "Pretty much all of his life savings. He's doing what he can, but he was never supposed to be involved with all of this—the tavern part, I mean. He's the brewer."

"We need to meet with him," Gwen said. "Whoever this guy is—and I assume it's an old friend of Dad's—he needs to step up."

"Maybe he wasn't supposed to be involved with this," Evie added, "but if he might lose everything, too, then he needs to *get* involved."

"It's Lane," Mal blurted out. "Lane Thompson is our brewer."

As that bit of news settled, Gwen thought back over all the conversations she'd had by phone and email with her parents, and sometimes Mallory. *The partner. The brewer. Him. He.* She realized now none of them had ever used his name.

"Dad went into business with my ex-husband?" Evie asked, and then silence filled the room as even

Mallory didn't seem to know what to say. "You can't be serious."

"They always got along, honey, and years ago, when they discovered they both loved craft brewing, they became good friends," Ellen said quietly. "And all that was so long ago, he didn't think you'd mind."

All that meaning Evie and Lane's marriage and subsequent divorce. And if they were so sure Evie wouldn't mind, Gwen thought, they probably would have mentioned his name at some point in the last two or more years since they hatched this plan.

"If he didn't think I'd mind, why did he hide it?"

"I'm sorry, Evie," Mal said. "Dad wanted to find the right time to tell you, but he didn't want to spoil the holidays and that's pretty much the only time you come home, so…"

"Yeah, it's totally my fault none of you told me Dad and my ex were business besties," Evie snapped.

"Girls," Ellen said in a pleading tone. "It's my fault."

"It's Dad's fault," Gwen snapped, and they all fell silent as they tried to reconcile anger with grief.

"We can do this," Mallory said. "People start breweries all the time. If other people can do it, so can we."

"We don't have any choice," Gwen said. "Where do we start?"

"Case is coming over tomorrow to look things over, and I have a few things I'm going to ask him to help with to save us some money," Ellen said. "He's been such a help around here since your dad passed, and I hate to ask him, but for us and for Lane, he'll help out."

Gwen had stopped processing the words her mother was saying as soon as Case Danforth's name came out of her mouth. She was too busy making sure she revealed no reaction whatsoever to mention of the boy next door. Or man across the street, as the case may be.

She couldn't remember a time she hadn't had a crush on Casey "don't call me that" Danforth. Younger Gwen had mooned over his shaggy brown hair and dark eyes. Adult Gwen liked the way he kept it trimmed now, though it was still thick enough so her fingers itched to bury themselves in it. Just a little shy of six feet, he was what she considered a perfect height, and working outdoors kept him strong, lean and sun-kissed.

But she'd always been awkward around boys—even ones who were practically part of the family thanks to proximity and parental friendships—and then he asked Mallory to the winter carnival dance the year they were juniors and Mal was a sophomore.

Gwen had hidden her broken heart and never let on how wrenching it was to see her sister and the boy of her dreams together. And even once they'd broken up, Case remained forever off-limits to her. He was her sister's first love. Okay, maybe not first *love*. They'd been kids, but they had dated almost a year. She couldn't date her sister's ex, regardless.

But the crush remained, held in check largely thanks to the fact she'd rarely seen him since she'd moved out of Stonefield over fifteen years ago.

But whenever she *was* in town, she was aware that ember had never gone totally cold. Even during her last visit—the darkest days of her life—when he'd offered a comforting hug, she'd been aware of how good it felt to have his arms around her.

If Case was going to be crossing the street all the time, working with them to dig her mother and sister out of the hole her dad had left them in, she was going to have to make sure that ember didn't flare up into an active flame again.

Her feelings for Case Danforth were a secret she had no intention of sharing.

Chapter Two

We want to give a grateful shout-out to D&T Tree Service for trimming the trees in the square so our little town will look its best for our annual Old Home Day festivities, honoring the New England tradition of celebrating our hometowns. And nobody wants a repeat of 1997, when a tree branch fell on the maple syrup vendor's cart. Thankfully, nobody was hurt, but everybody who tried to picnic that year might remember the ensuing invasion of ants. Anyhow, thank you to Case Danforth and Lane Thompson for doing their part to keep Stonefield beautiful!

—Stonefield Gazette *Facebook Page*

Lane showed up for the breakfast meeting as promised, but Case wasn't surprised when his cousin
took off as soon as their business was finished. He
claimed he had too much work to do on the pile of
town, state and federal paperwork necessary to make
and sell an alcoholic beverage, and Case believed
that. But he also knew that Mallory and Ellen had
probably told Evie who David's partner was by now.
He'd always felt that was a ridiculous thing to keep
a secret, but it had mattered to her dad, so they'd all
kept their mouths shut. He couldn't imagine that rev-
elation had gone over well.

After he'd cleaned up the breakfast mess, he took
Boomer outside to do his business. Once the dog was
done and appeared to be contemplating a good place
for his third nap of the day, Case told him they were
going to see Ellen and he perked up.

They crossed the street, and Boomer wasted no
time bounding up the front steps. By the time Case
caught up with him, the ornate front door with its
fancy stained glass inset was opening.

He was expecting Ellen or Mal, but it was Gwen
who opened the door, and then she froze. "Oh. I
didn't hear you knock."

"Because I hadn't yet."

"Oh," she said again, and he smiled. For a woman
who made her living with words, she was working
with a pretty limited vocabulary this morning. "I

was just going to take a look around the carriage house while I wait for Mom to finish getting ready."

"I'll go with you." They started across the yard and, when he looked back, he saw that Boomer was content to sprawl on the porch and nap while waiting for a more interesting offer to come along. The massive porch on the old Queen Anne–style home offered protection from the cold wind in the winter and deep shade in the summer, so it was the dog's usual spot whenever Case was helping the Suttons with something outdoors.

With its cream siding and green trim and shutters, the Sutton house loomed large in a neighborhood of two-story capes like his own. It was a beautiful old house kept in good repair, and the carriage house that sat next to it—separated by a large, paved parking area and a lawn—was as beautiful. It was painted green with cream trim to complement the house, and was larger than many of the homes around them.

Inside, it wasn't so beautiful right now. When he opened the door and flipped the light on, he heard Gwen's quiet groan and sympathized. David and Lane had gutted the cavernous space, right down to the studs, and the only part they'd put an effort into putting back together as of yet was the back wall. The stairs down to the cellar—where the magic happened—were cut off from the rest of the room by a glass wall with a pass-coded door that kept the space open and lit while keeping the stairs inaccessible to the public. Or more accurately, to anybody who wasn't Lane. Shelves on the back wall behind the glass would display vintage brewing equipment David had collected over the years.

"It's not as bad as it looks," he reassured her. "Except for that strip down that right-hand wall and the restroom in that corner to the left of the back door, this is going to be open space with tables, anyway, so the lighting will be most of the work and expense, and the plumbing and appliances, of course."

"There was talk of a menu. Where's the kitchen?"

"See that area marked off by studs? The bar will go down the wall and end at the start of the kitchen."

When she turned to face him, her *are you kidding me?* look was clear in the harshness of the temporary work lights, and he couldn't really blame her. "That's it? That's not a very big kitchen."

"It's not a full restaurant menu, though. No burgers or steaks or any of that, so no commercial grill equipment, with the exhaust hoods and expense all that entails." He found it a little odd she hadn't been in the carriage house. It had to have been almost a year before David passed that they started gutting it. "Your dad worked on this for a long time. You never got a tour or saw plans?"

"No, I didn't. Dad wanted us to stay out until the big reveal, when it looked like his vision. And we were busy celebrating holidays or…"

The words trailed away, but Case knew how that sentence ended. *Burying my father.*

"Is the upstairs cleaned out, too?" she asked instead. "I'm surprised he didn't open up the ceiling some."

"It's pretty rough up there. Your parents have stuck a lot of stuff up there for storage over the years. They decided it would be easy to regulate the temperature in a space this big and open if they kept the existing ceiling, and the plan is for it eventually to be turned into the office."

"What about the addition my dad put on the back?"

"That's where the grain and a bunch of other stuff is being stored because it has the big garage door. I don't have the code on the door to the cellar or I'd give you a tour. Mostly it's a lot of big metal tanks that do different things, and part of the space was sectioned off as a cold room."

"Do they expect a server to run up and down those stairs a hundred times a night, getting beer?"

The sharpness in her tone made him want to tease her. Tell her that now she knew why Mallory had asked her to come home—somebody had to carry mugs of beer up and down the stairs. But he restrained himself for now because this was a lot for her to process and he didn't think she'd appreciate the humor right now. "The beer will go into kegs, and lines run from the kegs to the taps the server at the bar will use. I guess you don't spend a lot of time in taprooms."

She just shook her head as she looked around the carriage house, and he wasn't sure if she was trying to imagine what it might look like finished, or if she was silently fuming. Knowing Gwen as he did, probably a little of both.

"Tell me something, Case," she said, fixing her pretty blue eyes on him. "What made my dad so sure this could work?"

"Maybe because there's nothing like it in Stonefield. It fills a need."

She tilted her head and Case had to bite back a smile because Boomer did the same thing when he was confused. "What do you mean?"

"We have the diner, of course. It's pretty much the culinary hub in this town, but they don't serve alcohol. The pizza house doesn't have a liquor license anymore. There's the new breakfast café, but I'm not sure how long that'll last because it's the kind of place where it takes five minutes just to read the fancy coffee options, and they definitely don't have beer. Aunt Daphne said she had to do a Google search for half the menu items because she'd never heard of them. And we do technically have a bar, but it's like eight seats in the middle of a chain restaurant, so you've got a family celebrating a kid's birthday on one side of you and the pastor and his wife sharing appetizers on the other. There's no place to go and just have a beer with your friends. Maybe let loose a little."

"But not too loose, since it's literally in my mother's yard."

"You don't sound very happy about that."

"Are you happy about it? It's going to be across the street from your bedroom window."

A memory from a long time ago surfaced in Case's mind, making him chuckle. Back when he'd been dating Mallory, she'd complained that Gwen had the street-facing room because if Mal's bedroom windows had faced his, she could have drawn hearts on the glass for him. Instead, his window faced Gwen's and if she was going to be in town for a while, he should probably start closing his curtains.

He wondered if Gwen would close hers and then wanted to kick himself. Whether she did or not, he wasn't going to try to peek. One, that would be creepy as hell, and two, it was Gwen. He'd never been into Gwen that way.

"The plans deliberately keep it small," he said, determined to get his thoughts back on track, "so it shouldn't be too rowdy, except maybe during sports playoffs. And your dad and Lane spent considerable time talking about the balance between being affordable in this area versus keeping the prices high enough to keep out the people just looking to get drunk."

"And the parking?"

"The back lawn, behind the carriage house, is being turned into a parking lot. You guys never use it, anyway, and it will connect with the other street, so cars won't be going in and out of your mom's driveway." He shoved his hands in the pockets of his jeans. "I know it's probably a lot to take in, but they really put a lot of thought and care into it. Once you've seen all the plans and talk to Lane, I think you'll feel better about the whole thing."

"If they were bound and determined to do it, I guess it wouldn't have made sense to buy or lease another property when Dad had this, but it's weird to have it so close."

"How come Ellen never moved the thrift store into the carriage house? It seems like it would have been easier, especially when you were kids."

"She inherited the business—and the building— from *her* parents, even though she changed the name to Sutton's Seconds after they passed because she hated the word *junk* in the original name. My grand-parents chose that location because it's in the sight line and easy walking distance of the market, which has the highest foot traffic in town. And I think she liked the distance. When she was at work, she was *at work*. If the thrift store was here, she probably would have spent half her time running between the shop and the house."

"She's a smart woman."

"She is." Gwen sighed. "Which is why I can't be-lieve she let Dad get in this deep. How could she let him do this?"

"Because it was his dream and I loved him."

Case winced when Ellen's voice echoed through the space. He hadn't heard her come in, and obvi-ously Gwen hadn't, either. The carriage house was suddenly the last place he wanted to be, but Ellen was between him and the door, so all he could do was give Gwen what he hoped was a sympathetic look and pretend to be interested in the electrical wires.

"I'm sorry, Mom." Gwen decided it was best to lead with that. "I didn't mean for that to sound as harsh as it did. I'm still trying to wrap my head around all of this and it's a lot."

"I know it is, honey. But it really was a solid plan right up until he went and died on us." Ellen sniffed and took a second to compose herself before giving Gwen a smile. "We're all still grieving, which we'll do in different ways, and now we have all of this to deal with, so I think the most important thing we can do is be quick with forgiveness. We need each other now and we're going to get through it together."

Gwen nodded, thankful for the sentiment, even though it didn't erase the fact she'd hurt her mother's feelings. But Ellen had raised three daughters and gotten out of the habit of taking things too personally a long time ago, so they'd move on. Gwen just needed to be more careful choosing her words in the future.

"Who's the contractor?" she asked, ready to get back to the business at hand. It was pretty clear from the scope of the work being done that they'd needed a professional.

Ellen sighed. "Mostly your father."

Before Gwen could let loose the curse word that was floating in her mind, Case reentered the conversation. "I'm pretty handy. So is Lane. I think we can handle a lot of the basic stuff."

Ellen shook her head. "I have a few things I was hoping you could help with so we wouldn't have to pay a contractor, but they're little things and I don't want to take up more time than that because you boys have your own business to run."

"So we'll multitask for a while. We've got a good crew, so we can sneak some time away when we need to. And there are evenings and weekends, since neither of us have significant others at the moment."

Case was single. Gwen hadn't realized her subconscious had been mulling over that very question until the answer flooded her with a rush of pleasure at knowing that little fact. Having a crush she couldn't shake on her sister's first real boyfriend was bad enough. She did *not* want to have a crush on another woman's man.

Of course, in an ideal world, she wouldn't be attracted to Case at all. But currently, nothing about her life was ideal.

"I hate asking that much of you," Ellen said, but Gwen could see the relief on her mom's face. Maybe, more than anything, Ellen just needed to know she wasn't alone. Considering Gwen's skill set, that was about *all* she could do, so she made up her mind to stop thinking about Case, stop resenting having to be back in Stonefield—for a little while, at least—and be as helpful to her mother as she could.

Then Case bent over to pick up a stray nail, pulling his jeans tight across an exceptionally nice ass, and Gwen revised her brand-new resolution. She would only think about Case *sometimes*, and preferably only when she was alone in her room at night. And definitely not when her overly observant mother was nearby, because Ellen had seen her checking out Case's butt and gifted her with an arched eyebrow that made Gwen's face feel even warmer.

She kept her mouth shut as she followed along behind Ellen and Case as her mom asked him questions about some of the decisions David had made and asked his opinion on some of the decisions *yet* to be made.

"I didn't even think to bring a notebook out with me," Ellen said after a while. "I should go get one and write this all down."

They all left the carriage house together, but when her mom went into the house to dig up something to write on, Gwen sat down in one of the porch rocking chairs with a sigh. Boomer looked up at her, but didn't bother getting up to lie at her feet, maybe deciding she wasn't a good bet for head scratches or belly rubs. Gwen was a little put out by his lack of faith in her.

But then Case sat in one of the other chairs, close enough to touch—not that she was going to—and the dog didn't bother to move for him, either, which made her feel better. Rocking back in the chair, she breathed in the fresh air and sighed. "I do miss this porch sometimes."

"It's a beautiful spot, for sure," Case responded, and Gwen winced because she hadn't meant to say that out loud. "You don't live *that* far away. How come we don't see you more often?"

"I like where I live." That wasn't much of an answer, so she wasn't surprised when Case just waited—letting the silence go on until it was awkward, and she sighed. "You might have heard about a book called *A Quaking of Aspens*?"

"Don't tell me you avoid this town because of that?" He snorted. "People get riled up over the dumbest things. You shouldn't let people's thoughts on your book keep you from your family."

"I talk to my family all the time."

"It's not the same as seeing them."

Gwen was quiet as the sharp pang of guilt over missing last Christmas with her dad hit again before slowly fading back to its usual dull ache. "No, it's not. But you have no idea how annoying it is that people in this town think the book is about *them.* Like it's the Stonefield version of *Peyton Place*, or something. And it finally started to die down and then they made the movie. And then the movie started getting nominated for awards, and I literally couldn't go to the market without hearing about it. That's when I decided it was time to find a new town to live in."

"Most people think you felt like you were too big a deal to live here anymore."

She snorted. "I just wanted to put gas in my car

without Bob complaining to me that his gas station is *not* run-down and has more than one gas pump, no matter how many times I told him it was a fictional gas station and not actually his."

"Come to think of it, I *have* heard people insinuate the guy who swept the protagonist off her feet was meant to be Tony Bickford." She snorted again, which made him grin. "Tony always wears a Red Sox hat. The guy in the book always wears a Red Sox hat."

"We live in New England, Case. You can't swing a bat without hitting a guy wearing a Red Sox hat."

"So not Tony, then?"

"No." She didn't want to talk about this anymore. "Of course Mrs. Bickford didn't believe that and refused to speak to me after the book released."

"You did kill off her son in a horribly tragic accident."

She might have been annoyed if not for the impish gleam in his eye. "He shouldn't have hit me in the face playing dodgeball in fourth grade gym class."

Let them all believe it was Tony Bickford, she told herself. As long as nobody guessed it was Case she'd pictured in her mind while writing that book, she didn't care what they thought. And as for the horribly tragic accident, maybe her inspiration should have asked Gwen to the winter carnival dance instead of Mallory.

Then, no matter how hard she pressed her lips

together, she couldn't stop herself from asking the question. "Did you read it?"

He chuckled, and her heart sank as she anticipated him trying to come up with all kinds of excuses as to why he hadn't read the book that made her a literary household name almost overnight. Or the two books she'd had published since, to significantly less acclaim.

"Of course I read it," he finally said. "I've read them all."

Warmth spread through her, and she was uncomfortably aware that he could probably see it on her cheeks. But there was nothing she could do to stop it, because all her mind wanted to do was wallow in the satisfaction that Case Danforth had read all of her books.

"I usually read nonfiction stuff and maybe a few thrillers here and there, but you're a damn good writer and the setting was so real, I could imagine myself in it." He paused and then grinned. "Maybe because I actually live here."

She reached out and slapped his arm, but she couldn't help laughing and he joined in. It felt so good to laugh. Living alone, a book or movie would sometimes make her chuckle. On the rare occasion she went out with friends or attended a social event, she was usually quiet and content to let the others do the talking and laughing. She almost never really, truly laughed except when she was with family or lifelong friends she was comfortable with.

Lifelong friends like Case Danforth, apparently.

"I guess I missed something," Ellen said as she stepped out onto the porch. "But I did find a new notebook that I can use just for the brewery so I don't miss any of *that*."

Gwen almost asked where her dad's notebook was. She remembered him scribbling in an old leather journal sometimes, when he had thoughts on a new beer he'd tried or ideas for interesting flavors. It contained many years' worth of planning for what they were trying to do here, so she was a little surprised she hadn't seen it. But her mom was writing in her spiral-bound notebook and Gwen didn't want to interrupt her train of thought, so she didn't ask about it. Maybe it was too painful for her mom to add notes where her husband had left off.

While Case very patiently went over everything they'd talked about for a second time, Gwen felt herself relaxing and taking in her surroundings. The low timbre of his voice. The comfort of the shade as the morning sun started heating up the yard. And Boomer, who decided to get up and lumber over for ear scratches. He propped his chin on her knee and gazed up at her adoringly while she scratched the top of his head, and he was so cute Gwen couldn't help turning to smile at the dog's human.

Case was smiling, too. While Ellen bent over the notebook on her lap, scribbling notes, he was watching her, and Gwen couldn't force herself to look away when his dark gaze locked with hers. His eyes crinkled at the corners, and she shivered at the heat she imagined she saw there—there was definitely something different in the way he was looking at her.

Then Boomer nudged her hand and she realized she'd stopped scratching, so she tore her attention away from the man and turned it back to the dog.

Nope, she wasn't going to think about Case and his laugh and his eyes and the way he'd just looked at her. She wasn't going to think about it at all.

Chapter Three

It's the final week of school, Stonefield! With summer vacation almost upon us, we have a couple of bargains to share with our readers to help you be prepared. Sutton's Seconds is taking 20% off their outdoor toys, as well as 10% off video games and DVDs, so head to the thrift store for summer entertainment. And Dearborn's Market has BOGO deals on popsicles, as well as deep discounts on Tylenol and wine, so stock up now!

—Stonefield Gazette *Facebook Page*

Gwen stared up at the glow-in-the-dark stars she'd stuck on her ceiling at some point during her middle school years, listening to the thump of footsteps and the yelling about homework and then the louder yelling about what was going to happen to the video game console if the boys were late to school again.

Usually her mornings consisted of brewing herself a mug of coffee and sitting at the table with her journal, reviewing her notes from the day before and writing out what she wanted to accomplish for the day. Shouting and banging and stars that had stopped glowing years ago—though she had to admire the longevity of the adhesive—were never part of the routine.

After she heard the boys' voices on the sidewalk outside her window—which faced the street and the Danforth house—she threw back the covers and got ready to face her morning. Her journal was still in her bag and she didn't bother digging for it. While she was going to get the coffee part of the ritual, she had no doubt peace and quiet would be in short supply.

Meanwhile, her beautiful and modern condo was sitting empty and silent, except for the cleaning service she'd asked to go from visiting weekly to every two weeks while she was away. And her neighbor would be gathering her mail—which she didn't get a lot of, other than junk, thanks to doing everything online—and letting Gwen know if anything looked important.

For now, she'd be making do in her beautiful but very unmodern childhood home. The DIY makeover had taken her parents so long that by the time they finished, the rooms they'd started with were already outdated. The kitchen had a second refresh in 2005 and it would probably live in that decade for a long time.

One of the benefits of growing up in a house that had once been a very upscale inn was that her room had its own bathroom, as did Mallory's. Evie, being the youngest, shared a bathroom between her room and the rarely used guest room, which was almost as good. Those two rooms were Jack's and Eli's now, and she realized as she showered that she had no idea where Evie had slept.

She'd told her parents several times that keeping the largest of the rooms—outside of the master suite, of course—for her was ridiculous because she rarely slept in it and Mallory actually lived in the house. But Mallory said she was content with the arrangement as it was and didn't care to move everything around, and their mother seemed to take some pleasure out of making sure they all still felt like the house was their home.

Except for Evie, she thought. Maybe they'd temporarily put the boys in one room and given Evie hers back, but Gwen knew she should at least ask. Although, knowing her youngest sister, she probably just crashed on the couch or curled up in her ancient Jeep. That go-with-the-flow attitude that often grated on Gwen's nerves did come in handy sometimes.

When she reached the kitchen, desperate for a shot of caffeine, she found Mallory sitting at the table with her hands curled around a mug, just staring into the steaming liquid. "Good morning."

"Morning, Gwen." She looked up and Gwen frowned when she saw how exhausted her sister looked. "Did you sleep okay?"

"Not bad," she lied as she poured herself a cup of coffee from the carafe. Not finding half-and-half in the fridge was a disappointment, but at least she'd have caffeine. "How about you?"

Mal shrugged one shoulder. "I don't sleep all that great anymore. There's a lot going on, you know?"

The guilt washing over her took some of the joy out of her first sip of coffee—though it would have been better with the half-and-half—and Gwen sat across from her sister. "We're here to help now. I'm sorry it wasn't sooner."

"You didn't know how bad it was. We didn't, either, at first. Going through everything takes time and then researching options takes time, and now it's been six months and it's a hot mess." She pushed her thick blond hair back from her face and blew out a breath. "I don't know what's going to happen, Gwen."

"We're going to make it work." But the doubt she felt was mirrored on her sister's face, so she decided to throw some truth into the mix. "But look, if it doesn't, and everything falls apart, then we find a small house or an apartment to rent for you guys and life will go on."

"Honestly? There have been a few times over the

last six months that I really felt that was the best option—to leverage whatever we could to save the thrift store's building. I would really hate to evict the upstairs tenant, but Mom, Jack and Eli are my priority. And it would suck because it's a two bedroom, but if Mom and I shared one room and the boys the other, we could make it work." She chuckled. "Trust me, my initial goal was focused—out of all of the mess—on how to save *that* property. But Mom just came totally undone."

"That's understandable. She just lost her husband, so the idea of losing her *home* is probably overwhelming. That doesn't mean it's not the best option, though."

"Except Dad mortgaged that building, too, and because it's pretty prime downtown commercial real estate—even here in Stonefield—they valued it high and it's a lot of money. If we lose the building, the thrift store probably couldn't support the rent a new owner would charge. And there's Lane, too. I know he chose to take the risk, but we still don't want *him* to lose everything, too. I mean, he'd still have half the tree service because he didn't want to involve Case, but his house and his savings are tied up in the brewery."

Gwen tried to ignore the way her heart did a little stutter step when Mal said Case's name. "Then it sounds like our only option is to make this work. Welcome to the beer business, I guess."

Mal smiled and held out her mug, and Gwen

gently clinked hers against it just as Evie walked into the kitchen. She was wearing a tank top and men's boxer shorts, and with her tousled hair and chipper morning attitude, she made Gwen feel a hundred years old.

"What are we toasting to?" Evie asked, rummaging around in the fridge until she found a bottle of orange juice. After sniffing it—Ellen wasn't great with expiration dates, so they'd all learned young to check for themselves—she poured herself a glass and sat down.

"Our resolve to being the best beer brewers that Stonefield has ever seen," Mal said.

"Technically we already are, since we're the first," Evie said, and then she held out her glass for another toast. "Hell yes to a goal already met!"

They all laughed, and Gwen let herself savor the shared amusement with her sisters. There probably wasn't going to be a lot of good cheer in their very near future, so they might as well enjoy it while it lasted.

"Did you sleep in your old room?" Gwen asked, since it had been on her mind.

Evie nodded. "The boys are bunking together and the three of us are sharing the bathroom, which is… fun."

That made them all laugh again, but if any of them were suited to sharing a bathroom with eight- and ten-year-old boys, it was Evie. Not only was she the most easygoing of them, but she had a lot of experience with sharing space with random roommates.

"Where's Mom?" Evie asked.

"She left for the thrift store already," Mal said.

"Isn't it closed on Mondays?"

"She wanted to cull some things to donate because they haven't sold." Mal paused for a few seconds and gave a weary sigh. "This has been a lot for her and even though she's thrilled you're both here, it makes everything feel even more intense and urgent. She's been… I wouldn't say hiding, but she's definitely been taking comfort from the shop the last few months. She spends a lot more time there than I do."

"Speaking of both of us being here," Gwen said, "where have you been living, Evie? We got here at almost the same time."

"Weird, huh?" Evie shrugged. "I was in Maryland for a few weeks. They have ponies that run wild on the beach and I got some great pictures. When I get time, I'll tweak them a bit and throw them on my Etsy shop."

"That's an expensive area to live," Mal said, her brows knitting together.

"You're telling me. I was bartending at a place on the beach and crashing with some friends I met there. But I was ready to move on anyway because one of the guys was starting to think I'd be a cool girlfriend even though I wasn't into him, and you know how that goes."

Gwen sipped her coffee and kept her mouth shut

while Mallory asked a few questions about the ponies. She *did* know how it went with Evie. Always on the move, doing whatever odd jobs kept food in her belly and her Jeep running. And while she had to admit her youngest sister had seen and experienced a lot of very cool things, Gwen thought it was well past time for her to at least be considering settling down somewhere.

"Have either of you seen Dad's notebook?" she asked when there was a lull in the conversation, because it had been on her mind. "The leather one? Does Mom have it tucked away somewhere?"

"I haven't seen it," Evie replied. "Which is weird, because it was always lying around somewhere."

"Lane has it." Mallory gave Evie an apologetic glance. "He asked Mom for it after the funeral and promised to give it back after the brewery is up and running."

Gwen wasn't sure how she felt about the journal being in somebody else's hands. "They did this together for years—talking about it and doing some hobby brewing—so why did he need it?"

"Lane never writes anything down," Evie said, and then she sighed, as if annoyed that she still remembered her ex-husband's quirks.

"I'm sure he's keeping it safe because it probably means almost as much to Lane as it does to us," Mal said. "And in a slight change of subject, Mom threw a curveball at me as she was leaving this morning. I'm pretty sure she timed it that way, knowing I'd have my hands full getting the boys out the door. It's the Monday of their last week of school and they're well past ready for summer vacation to start."

"Mom's curveball?" Gwen prompted, before they went too far down a conversation detour about the kids.

"We're hosting a barbecue tonight."

"Cool." Evie said. "I could go for a burger."

Gwen gave her a look that often resulted in her youngest sister sticking out her tongue in response, but apparently Evie had evolved into just rolling her eyes. "So setting aside that it's weird to be hosting a barbecue on a Monday night…if we're the hosts, who are the guests?"

Mal stared into her coffee for a few seconds. "Lane and Case are coming over so we can have a group discussion. She said it's time to stop trying to convince them everything's just peachy keen over here. We're all in this together and we have to start acting like it."

"Case really isn't in it, though," Gwen protested, belatedly realizing it was an odd thing to say, since Case's presence wasn't the most important information Mallory had relayed.

Mal shrugged. "He's Lane's cousin, business partner—though a different business, of course—his best friend, and he lives across the street and helps us out with a bunch of things. He's not going to be able to keep himself out of it, and we need all the help we can get."

"So Lane's coming here for dinner tonight is what you're telling us," Evie said, her usual effervescence seemingly muted somehow.

"Are you okay with that?"

Evie sighed. "I have to be, don't I?"

Even her many years of experience in being the big sister didn't help Gwen come up with a response. Evie was right, and she didn't really have a choice about it. Thanks to their dad, her ex-husband was going to be all up in their lives and business for quite some time, and there was nothing anybody could do about it.

While Mal and Evie talked about Lane, Gwen's mind wandered to their other guest for the evening. In the rush and annoyance of packing up what she needed and getting back to Stonefield, she hadn't given a lot of thought to just how much time Case spent at the Sutton house. Avoiding him was easy when she was only in town for a couple of days to visit her parents and get out again. She wasn't going to be able to avoid him this time.

But if Evie could work alongside her ex-husband, Gwen could work alongside a longtime family friend she'd had a crush on growing up. She'd pretend she hadn't felt anything yesterday, definitely not think about the way he'd looked at her, and ignore any tingling and yearning that might pop up in the future.

She was a grown woman now and she absolutely could not be attracted to Case Danforth anymore. It was that simple. He'd dated her sister. He had very deep roots in this town she couldn't wait to get out of. There was already too much on her plate, and she didn't have time for misguided entanglements.

It was time to outgrow the childhood crush she'd never been able to shake. She'd outgrown *Beverly Hills, 90210,* as well as a steady diet of frosted toaster pastries and soda.

She could outgrow Case.

"You ready for this?"

When Lane made a growling sound deep in his throat, Case took that as a *hell no.* But Ellen hadn't been wrong about the need to bring them all together so they could be on the same page as they worked toward a common goal.

"At least there will be burgers," he said to Lane, but it was the dog who picked up his head and looked excited at the prospect. "Yes, Boomer. You know Ellen always makes you a burger of your own, hold the pickles."

Since David died, Case had done what he could across the street. Using David's old tractor to clear the snow. Then changing out the attachment when it was time to mow the extensive lawns. Lugging mulch for the garden beds. Odd repairs. Replacing a ceiling fan. And not only did Ellen not have cash to spare, but Case wouldn't have accepted it from his neighbor anyway. He was raised better than that. But he didn't turn down free food, and Ellen was a damn good cook. Boomer wasn't great at the working part, but he was Case's sidekick, so he always got a treat, too.

"I was already over there for several hours today," Lane pointed out.

"Yeah, but you parked over here and went in through the back door of the carriage house to lock yourself in the brewing room, so they probably didn't even know you were there," Case countered. "And Ellen and Mallory would have been at the thrift store, so it wouldn't have been much of a group meeting."

"Now that Gwen's here, you know she's going to take over, anyway."

"She'll probably try." She'd always been the bossy one. He was an only child, but he'd gotten the impression over the years that it was a personality trait that came with being the first kid born. "But you're the only one in this little group who actually knows how beer is made, so you're definitely the one in charge."

"I wonder how Evie feels about me being involved."

Case could tell by the clenched jaw and stiff shoulders that Lane didn't think she'd be very happy about it. But he and David had known that was a possibility going in, and there was nothing that could be done about it now, so he shrugged. "I guess we'll find out if you ever stop stalling and put your shoes on."

"Fine."

They paused in the yard to let Boomer have a few minutes before crossing the street. Somebody—probably Mallory—had already fired up the grill, so he took that as a sign they'd eat before they got down to business. That worked for Case. He was starving, along with being a little sore. He and the crew that worked for them had to step it up a bit now that Lane was essentially working half days. They weren't falling behind, but it wasn't going to be long before they'd have to consider hiring on another guy. Especially since he'd told Ellen he could volunteer more of his own time.

"Boomer!" Both of Mallory's boys spotted the dog at the same time, and Case smiled as his dog ran off to get belly rubs that would surely be followed by chasing sticks and whatever balls they could scrounge up. Their mother wasn't up to getting them a dog because it would just be home alone all day, so Jack and Eli soaked up all the time with Boomer they could get.

It was the laugh that yanked his attention away from the boys and his dog. *Her* laugh.

He turned to the porch just as Gwen stepped through the door, holding a tray of uncooked burgers and laughing with Mallory, who was right behind her with a spatula and a bag of buns.

Gwen was wearing those summer pants that ended halfway down her very shapely calves, with a loose, flowered tank top that showed off skin that either rarely saw the sun or saw a *lot* of sunscreen. Her hair wasn't free, but it was pulled back so loosely that it still framed her face.

"You okay?" Lane asked, and he realized he'd not only stopped walking but was staring at Gwen.

"Yeah." He forced a chuckle. "I'm hungry and she's carrying a plate of burgers."

Lane's gaze bounced between Case and Gwen before his mouth quirked up in a half grin. "Sure. But those burgers are still raw, so put your tongue back in your mouth."

What am I doing? That was Gwen Sutton he'd been staring at. The bossy girl from across the street. The older sister of the girl he'd taken to winter carnival and… Well, more. There was a lifetime of reasons she wasn't his type. Sure, she was attractive. And she had that laugh. But it was Gwen, and what was he even thinking?

"Boys," Ellen called from the backyard, because it didn't matter how old they were. The Sutton sisters were her *girls*, and he and Lane would always be the *boys*. "The burgers won't take long, but there are some chips and salads in the gazebo if you're hungry."

A big perk of the Sutton house having once been an inn was the gazebo in the backyard that overlooked the river. It was a big one, meant to accommodate wedding photos and such, back in the day. Now it accommodated a long picnic table and the Suttons ate a lot of their meals there. David had suggested screening it in more than once, but Ellen insisted it would feel too closed in and defeat the purpose of eating outdoors, to say nothing of impeding the view.

Once he and Lane were in the gazebo, each with a first helping of macaroni salad, he tilted his head toward the grill, where all four Sutton women had gathered. While he'd be content to eat his food and watch Gwen, tension was emanating from Lane so strongly, Case could practically feel it pushing against him.

"You're going to have to talk to her at some point," he said, not bothering to clarify who *her* was.

"I know. It's not that big a deal," Lane replied, and Case wondered how his cousin managed to talk with his jaw clenched like that. "It's been a long time and we've both moved past it."

Case nodded, though he wasn't sure that was true. Evie hadn't looked in their direction once, and her sisters looked relaxed, but she certainly didn't. She looked almost as tense as Lane, and that was even more out of character for her than it was for him.

Two hours later, when they'd all eaten their fill, including Boomer, who was gifted half of Eli's burger in addition to his own, Case realized Evie and Lane still hadn't spoken directly to each other. With two kids and a dog running around and six adults trying to have something that resembled a business meeting, it was probably easy to hide from most of them, but he knew Evie was definitely not speaking to her ex-husband. And Lane was either too proud or too stubborn to break that awkward ice.

"Okay," Ellen said, setting her pen on top of her notebook with a sigh. "After everything is taken into consideration, the bottom line is that the brewery needs to be paying for itself by the end of the year or we're all in trouble. Making a profit would be nice, but the end of the year is when we'll start having to rob Peter to pay Paul, and Peter's got very shallow pockets."

Because he was sneaking yet another glance at Gwen, Case saw the way her expression tightened when Ellen said *the end of the year*, but she didn't say anything. The thought of staying in Stonefield for a month was probably enough to set her teeth on edge. But six months? She wasn't going to be happy about that.

But Case? He didn't think he was going to mind having Gwen around at all.

"Now." Ellen picked up her pen again. "We know what we have to do. Let's figure out how we're going to do it."

Chapter Four

The library will be holding their annual book sale on their lawn during the Old Home Day festivities! The proceeds will go toward fun activities for the Summer Reading Program, so if you'd like to donate books, drop them at the library during business hours. There will be several copies of A Quaking of Aspens *available for a dollar, but as you know, Gwen Sutton is in town. If she signs them, they'll be five dollars, so if you see her, be sure to tell her to grab a Sharpie!*

—Stonefield Gazette *Facebook Page*

Gwen didn't have a lot of experience with business meetings outside of the occasional lunch or dinner with her agent or editor, and the similarities between those and this one stopped at her getting a free meal. At least at *her* business dinners, there was almost always a cocktail involved.

She wasn't a big fan of beer. And she *really* wasn't a big fan of *talking* about beer. And sitting on a picnic table bench hadn't been a big deal when she was younger, but she wasn't a kid anymore. Her butt hurt and her back was protesting, and she was more focused on how her mother was tolerating the bench than she was on the so-called meeting.

"I don't think we'll have to hire any staff for quite some time," her mom was saying, and that got her attention because a business didn't run without staff. "Maybe even to the end of the year."

"Um," Gwen and Evie said together.

"I have a job," Gwen continued. "And I don't live here."

"I'm not staying that long," Evie said at the exact same time.

Gwen had known coming into this visit that it was going to be longer than she would like. She'd packed what she needed to get by, but she wanted to be back in Vermont by the end of the summer. Not only was she behind on her book, but fall and winter were her most productive times of the year. There was something about heading into the crispness of autumn that made her want to curl up with her laptop and write. The end of the year definitely didn't work for her.

"It's just for a little while," Ellen said, but her words weren't very reassuring, considering she'd just casually thrown out a six-month time frame. "We just have to figure out who's going to do what and work out the kinks before people start depending on us for their paychecks."

"I'm brewing the beer," Lane said, and Gwen threw him a look letting him know that, as far as she was concerned, that didn't let him off the hook for helping out wherever else he was needed.

"I already called dibs on not being the dishwasher," Evie reminded them.

"Obviously, you'll be the bartender, Evie." Ellen gave her youngest daughter a bright smile. "You have experience doing that, and you have the best personality for it."

Gwen stopped herself from rolling her eyes. That would be such an Evie thing to do.

When she felt a shoe tapping her ankle, she glanced around and it was Case who caught her attention. Not just because Case *always* caught her attention, but because he had his eyebrow raised and when their gazes locked, the foot tapped against her ankle again. Then he smiled.

Realizing he was letting her know that her less than positive thoughts about the current state of their business meeting were written all over her face, she smiled back. Probably not the most genuine smile she'd ever mustered, but it would have to do.

"Who's going to cook?" Mallory asked, and Gwen

lost the delicious eye contact with Case when they both turned to face her. "And before anybody answers that, I feel like now's a good time to remind everybody that I have been and will continue to do everything I can to help out, but I have kids and I work at the thrift store during the day and usually handle the online stuff in the evening so at least I'm home with them."

"You have online stuff?" Gwen interrupted.

"Yes, there's online stuff," Mallory replied, clearly exasperated by the derailing of the conversation. "There are some things that we can charge more for on the resale sites than we can get for them here in Stonefield and even with the shipping we make more of a profit. We live in the same century as everybody else, Gwen, and life keeps moving forward even if you're not here to see it."

Ouch. The pointed jab was so unlike Mal that it was practically a neon sign flashing Stressed to Capacity over her head. So Gwen shut down the part of her brain trying to compose a snarky response and said nothing.

"The seating capacity is limited, and it takes a while for a business to get rolling," Lane said, probably trying to get back on topic. "I think Evie can tend the bar and be the server."

"Sure," Evie snapped. "Let me just go dig out my old roller skates."

Nobody said anything, and Gwen realized those were the first words Evie had said to her ex-husband since finding out he'd been their dad's business part-

ner the entire time and nobody had told her. And as
her youngest sister glared at Lane, Gwen glanced
back at Case. He had his head bent, his thumb picking at the corner of the label on his empty water bottle. Then he looked up and their eyes met—lingering
there for a few seconds before he turned to Ellen.

"I have an idea," he said. "Lane said there wasn't
space or budget for a full kitchen or even for pizza
ovens, but maybe we can still offer that. When the
Stonefield House of Pizza lost their liquor license
several years ago because—well, I don't believe the
rumors about their son and the liquor commissioner's
wife—but anyway, they lost a lot of business. Guys
getting together after work for a beer and a pizza
couldn't have a beer. No beer with their wings on
a game day. Maybe we work a deal where we have
some basic appetizer stuff on-site, but we have a
partnership with the pizza place, where our customers can call and have something delivered here."

Gwen caught the *we* and *our* and realized just how
"in" Case was. He might not have money in the venture, but he was definitely invested.

"So they can have their pizza or wings and watch
a game and keep drinking the beer," Lane said, nodding. "I like it. And it takes a huge strain off of not
only the problem of who's doing what, but the budget."

"Gwen and I can probably handle the kitchen if
all we're doing is snack-type stuff at first," Ellen
said, tapping her pen on the table. "Eventually, when
money's being made, we can think about expanding

the food menu. Or maybe everybody will be happy with that arrangement and we'll just leave it alone."

Gwen and I. She thought about objecting—again— but it wouldn't do any good. And there wasn't only her mother to consider. Mallory was like a rubber band stretched to its limit and about to snap. They already knew Gwen wasn't staying forever. Reminding them of it every five minutes wasn't going to help.

Lane sighed, shifting on the picnic bench. "I can barely feel my legs anymore, so let's start wrapping this up. Tomorrow, Case and I have a meeting with the utility company about clearing the power lines, and since the guys will be doing an easy job in town, I asked the electrician to stop by in the afternoon. I looked over the bid he gave David and I'm going to knock that down some."

"I'll come, too," Case said, and Gwen bit back her smile. "The guys won't need me, and I can start making a more detailed supply list for Sheetrock and trim and all that."

"And we'll start brainstorming food ideas," Ellen said, making a note before closing the book. "Now, who's going to talk to Stonefield House of Pizza?"

"Not Gwen," they all said at the same time, and she groaned.

"Almost every single small town in New England has a something-House of Pizza," she said.

"That *was* a pretty graphic food poisoning scene," Evie said, laughing for the first time since they'd started the meeting.

"That wasn't even in my book," Gwen protested. "They added it to the movie version of *A Quaking of Aspens* for… I don't know why. Maybe audiences love vomiting."

"I'll talk to them," Mallory said, sounding tired. "Lord knows I'm there often enough grabbing pizzas for the boys lately."

"That's settled, then," Ellen said, standing up. With a groan and Case's hand at her elbow, she stepped over the bench and stretched her back. "Future meetings with be held in the kitchen so we can sit in proper chairs."

"I'll second that," Lane said, and Gwen saw him wince when he stood up.

The shuffling in the gazebo brought Boomer jogging over from the porch, where he'd been hanging out with Jack and Eli. Mallory had made them popcorn to go with the movie they wanted to watch outside on their mom's tablet, which had no doubt helped sway the dog's decision about who to hang out with. He went first to Case and then did a slow lap of the picnic table, probably disappointed to find it wasn't still laden with leftovers for him to beg.

It seemed as if the gazebo emptied in record time, because before she knew it, she was alone with Case. And unlike everybody else, he didn't seem to be in a hurry to leave.

"You looked like you were plotting how to murder some people," he said, his amusement obvious in his voice and the way the wrinkles at the corners of his eyes deepened. "You don't write murder mysteries, so I was getting a little worried."

That made her laugh and it eased some of the tension building inside of her. "I'll probably be writing horror by the time this is over."

They laughed together, and when the sound faded away, the eye contact remained. It was three breaths at least—heat seeping through her and probably flushing her cheeks—before he gave her a crooked smile and looked away.

How many years had she dreamed of him looking at her like that? And he waited until now, when she was hip deep in family drama and counting the days—or weeks, actually—until she could put it and this town behind her.

Maybe she was reading more into it, she told herself. He could have been thinking about something else, and the desire she'd seen in his eyes had been nothing but a figment of her overheated imagination.

"I guess I should go find Boomer," he said. "He went inside with the boys and he's had more than his limit of human food for the day."

"I should go help clean up," she said, but still neither of them moved, and he was looking at her that way again.

It definitely wasn't her imagination.

Case knew he couldn't kiss Gwen. For one thing, multiple windows of the house looked out over the gazebo, and anybody in the family could be watching at that moment.

For another, he just couldn't kiss her. Everything was a mess and getting involved with her would only tangle things up more. Even a temporary fling—and it would be temporary because she wasn't shy about how much she preferred being in Vermont—would make things worse. Or at the very least, more awkward.

Summoning every scrap of willpower he could muster, he jerked his head toward the house. "After you."

She'd probably assume it was the old *ladies first* rule, but mostly he just liked to watch her walk. He might have gathered up enough discipline not to kiss her, but he wasn't going to pass up an opportunity to admire the way her hips swayed as she crossed the yard.

Once they were inside, he looked for his dog but was informed the boys had smuggled him up to their room to keep them company while they theoretically cleaned it. They claimed having Boomer with them would make the chore more fun, but they all knew there would be more belly rubs than pulling of dirty socks out from under the bed.

Lane left right away—probably feeling uncomfortable being in the house while Evie was there and still not really speaking to him—but Case hung around to help clean up the stuff that had been brought in from the barbecue. Plus, he wasn't leaving without his dog.

After a half hour or so had passed, he realized he hadn't seen Gwen in a few minutes. He also hadn't heard anybody go up the old staircase with its distinctive creaks and squeaks, so he went looking for her. He didn't have to go far.

She was in the formal dining room, alone and standing with her hands on the back of a chair. While her gaze was on the table, he didn't think she was really seeing it. Either Gwen was getting worse at managing her facial expressions as she got older or Case had never really paid close enough attention to how readable her face really was. But he could tell she wasn't very happy at the moment.

"You know they don't really expect you to stay forever," he said in a low voice, which necessitated him walking close enough so he could smell her. She smelled mostly like sunscreen and a bug spray designed to smell better than it actually worked.

"In Stonefield time, six months *is* forever."

He laughed. "Come on. We're not that bad."

When she tilted her head and put her hands on her hips, he braced himself for a verbal blast. But she just glared at him for a few seconds before she spoke in a voice as low as his. "No, some of the people here aren't that bad."

Grinning, he nudged her shoulder with his. "How about me? How bad am I?"

It wasn't until the words had left his mouth that he realized that was a question that could be taken in a couple of ways. He hadn't intended any innuendo at all, but she might read some into the question. And when she glanced sideways at him, her eyebrow arched, he held his breath but she shook her head.

"You've been a pain in the ass since we were kids," she said, amusement in her voice. "But I guess you're not *that* bad."

It wasn't exactly high praise, but he'd take it. "Are you hiding in here to get out of the cleaning up?"

She chuckled. "Just having a few minutes of quiet time."

Stepping closer to the table, he looked at the jigsaw puzzle that was about half-done on the wooden surface. "There's usually a puzzle going in here. I've been known to pop a few pieces in now and again."

"You can tell Evie's been working on it because all the fun stuff in the middle is done and all that's left is the sky and the grass."

"Doesn't everybody do puzzles like that?" When she gave him a sideways look, he realized it was the wrong thing to ask. Maybe it *was* human nature to do the fun stuff and leave the boring and hard parts for somebody else, but it annoyed her more when it was Evie. They'd always been that way. "I remember the time your dad bought that puzzle that was just spilled milk or something?"

Gwen laughed. "I'd forgotten about that one. All the pieces were white—*all* of them—so all we had to go on was the shape. I hated that one."

"We all did."

She looked at him, her expression shifting to a

low-level scowl. "That's right. You were dating Mallory then, and I think you spent more time here than you did at your own house."

He suddenly realized—as if a cartoon light bulb had lit up over his head—that Gwen didn't like being reminded that he'd dated her sister in high school.

And that was very interesting to him. He knew, of course, that you weren't supposed to date your sibling's or best friend's ex, but he was pretty sure that didn't apply to relationships that happened while you were still kids. It was a small town. They all came out of high school with very tangled histories.

But, more importantly, he couldn't see a good reason why Gwen would be annoyed at the reminder he and Mallory had dated in high school, and what if it was because *she* wanted to date him herself?

"What?"

Jerked back to reality, he saw Gwen giving him a questioning look. "What?"

"You were looking smug about something—like *really* pleased with yourself—so what were you thinking about?"

Telling her the truth wasn't really an option he wanted to consider, so he shrugged. "I was just thinking about how I got more of that milk puzzle done than anybody else."

Her eyes widened. "You did not! You might have spent more time complaining about it than the rest of us, but you definitely didn't fit more pieces together."

As expected, his distraction worked and they debated who was better at puzzles for a bit. It wasn't him, since he usually got bored after a few minutes, but he didn't have to admit that. He preferred her fired up, with her eyes snapping and her lips curved in the thrill of debate.

"I think we were all relieved when it was gone," he admitted finally.

"That was funny," Gwen said, smiling at the memory. "Remember how Mom came in with the big Shop-Vac and said she was done listening to us whine about that stupid puzzle and just sucked all the pieces right off the table?"

"Along with the purple Skittles I was saving for last because they're the best flavor."

She snorted. "You should have thanked her because red Skittles are the best flavor."

As if he needed another reason to be attracted to Gwen. Sure, she was wrong about red being the best flavor, but that meant they could share a bag of Skittles without fighting over their favorites. Compatibility mattered.

"Gwen?"

Ellen's voice echoed through the house, and Gwen sighed. "I guess quiet time's over."

He started to back up so she could get by him, but not fast enough. Her body brushed his, and maybe it was his imagination, but she seemed to pause for a second, as if registering the full body contact. Then she was gone and Case was left alone to imagine all the ways that could have gone differently if her mom hadn't been waiting for her.

He could have wrapped his arms around her and pulled her up hard against him. Then he'd bury his face in her hair before kissing his way from her neck to her mouth. With that light, flowing shirt she was wearing, he could easily slide his hand up her back, feeling the heat of her skin under his hand.

This was definitely not the time or the place to continue that line of thinking. Maybe later, in the shower, would be good. For now, he needed to distract himself.

Case had put almost half the sky pieces together before he felt under control enough to join the others again.

Chapter Five

Just a friendly reminder that a line of cars pull-
ing out of Cyrs Funeral Home with their head-
lights on is a funeral procession, not a sports
victory parade. Please do not honk your horn
and pump your fist out the window.
—Stonefield Gazette *Facebook Page*

Gwen knew she couldn't put it off anymore. She was going to have to venture out into Stonefield and do some errands.

What she *should* do was write. She'd been in Stonefield for almost a week and hadn't yet. The laptop was sitting on the table next to the glider rocker she'd spotted at the thrift store when she was sixteen and begged for until her father went in and bought it from his own wife for her. It had been well-worn then and had turned the corner to shabby years ago, but it was comfortable, and sometimes when she was at home in the fancy power recliner she'd overpaid for, she felt a wave of nostalgia for the chair she'd written so many stories in.

Yet, here she was, and no writing was happening.

And she was totally blaming the lack of half-and-half in the house. Coffee with milk was okay in a pinch, but if she was going to be living here temporarily—though not as temporarily as she would have liked—there were some basic things she needed. And it didn't feel right to add them to the list on the fridge or ask her mom or Mal to pick them up. It was time to reacquaint herself with her hometown.

It was another half hour before she went downstairs, so her mother and Mallory and the boys were already gone. Evie was sitting at the kitchen table, though, and they muttered greetings as Gwen walked to the coffee maker and poured herself a cup. She put a little extra sugar in it to try to offset the plain milk and sat at the table.

Then she took a sip and grimaced. "I'm definitely going to the store today. Do you need anything?"

Evie snorted. "Going to buy some fancy espresso thing that foams milk and makes lattes or whatever?"

"Half-and-half. I just want some half-and-half, Evie. And don't do that."

"Don't do what?"

"Act like I'm a snob or whatever. I'm not."

"You make it very, very obvious you don't want to be here."

Two sips of winceworthy coffee were not enough caffeine for her to argue with Evie, but Gwen couldn't let that go. "You're never here, either."

Evie shrugged. "But you're not here because you don't want to be *here*. I'm not here because I want to be so many other places. There's a difference."

"No, there isn't. I'm not here because I want to be in Vermont. You want to be wherever you were, taking pictures of ponies." She took another sip of her coffee and then sighed. "I don't want to fight with you, Evie. Neither of us wants to spend who-knows-how-long in this town, but we don't have any choice. Taking it out on each other isn't going to make the time go by any faster."

"I don't want to fight with you, either."

For the first time, Gwen realized Evie was scrolling on her phone—which was pretty typical for her—but she also had a notebook next to her juice glass, which was different. "What are you doing?"

Evie shrugged one shoulder. "Looking at the social media feeds for some of the other small breweries in the state. Seeing what they're doing right and what they could be doing better."

"I guess social media will be a thing for us eventually." She wasn't a big fan, personally. It was harder for her to write when readers had immediate access to her.

"We should be doing it already," Evie said.

"Glimpses and teases and whetting their appetites for new brews to try and a fun place to hang out. Getting people excited about it is better than just 'oh hey, we're open now' because they'll talk about it and share and get *other* people excited."

Gwen followed her sister's social media accounts—trying not to be *too* envious of Evie's adventures and the gorgeous places she posted pictures from—and she had to admit her sister had a knack for it. She certainly knew more about it than the rest of them. Gwen posted pictures that inspired her or gave glimpses into her process and life so readers didn't forget her between books, but it wasn't specifically product marketing and she did the bare minimum.

"If you have ideas for it, you should start," Gwen said, and Evie looked surprised. "I think the fact nobody brought it up at all last night and you're already making notes proves you're the right woman for the job."

"Thanks."

"And you're really good at it."

Evie's face softened and she gave Gwen a warm smile. "Thanks. That means a lot."

Gwen drank her coffee and Evie sipped her juice for a few minutes, until the next question popped into Gwen's head. "Has anybody mentioned a name at all? For the brewery, I mean?"

"I don't think so. We need to find out if Dad or Lane had to put something on the paperwork. If we don't have a name yet, we need to do that next because we need a name to start social media accounts, and we'll need a logo for that, and for the sign and stickers."

"Stickers? You mean labels?"

"No, stickers. People who go around to different breweries like to collect stickers."

"Oh." She was definitely out of her depth here. "We should ask Lane."

Evie wrinkled her nose. "I think *you* should ask Lane."

"I honestly didn't know, by the way. That he's who Dad went into business with. I asked once and, thinking back, I didn't get a straight answer. I assumed it was somebody he'd met who I didn't know and I was busy and I guess I just didn't ask again."

"Same here. I wish Dad had told me, though. I would have had time *away* from here to process it and come to terms with it. Instead, I got blindsided." She set her phone down and folded her arms. "I'll get over it. I have to. But…it's not even so much that it's my ex-husband but more that Dad kept that secret from me. And Mom and Mal went along with it. Even after he died, I mean."

"I'm guessing Mom has had too many emotions on her plate to add a potential falling-out with you, and Mal… I don't know." That one was tougher because Mallory was Evie's sister. She should have told her. "She probably didn't want to add the two of you arguing onto Mom's plate, either."

Evie shrugged a shoulder. "Whatever. It's done."

"You want to go to the store with me?" Gwen asked, surprising herself with the invitation. And Evie, too, judging by the way her eyebrows arched. "We need to get out of this house, even for just an hour."

"I'm in."

Two hours later, they had a bunch of stuff they probably didn't need—they definitely didn't need the Oreos or party-size bag of Doritos—but they were enjoying the shopping and Gwen thought this was the most fun she'd had with Evie in a long time. It was a simple thing, but it felt good.

Then they turned a corner and Evie almost ran straight into Mrs. Dorsey with the shopping cart. Gwen braced herself as recognition dawned on the woman's face and her overly drawn eyebrows reached for her dyed-black hairline.

"Gwen Sutton," she said, her voice rough with age and decades of smoking. "I heard you were back."

"Hello, Mrs. Dorsey."

"You know, the actress who played me in the movie looked nothing like me. She was way too old, to begin with."

Stifling what would have been a long and very beleaguered sigh, Gwen resisted the urge to point out the actress in question was a good fifteen years younger than the woman in front of her. "She wasn't playing you, Mrs. Dorsey. You weren't in the movie because you weren't in the book."

"Of course I was. She worked at the town hall and the front door of her house was painted blue and everybody knows I painted my front door blue because it matched my new car."

Gwen was fairly certain she was already trying to find an agent for her completed manuscript when the Dorsey door was painted, but then she'd be stuck explaining how publishing worked and Mrs. Dorsey would only point out she could have added her in the revision stages. "A lot of people have blue doors."

Mrs. Dorsey sniffed. "At least I got to live to the end. Poor Tony."

She was still making that *tsk* noise and shaking her head when she walked away, and Gwen resisted the urge to abandon the cart and leave the store. People's reaction to thinking they were in her book hadn't been as bad over her last several visits as it had been in the months following *A Quaking of Aspens'* release, though she hadn't gone into town a lot and her last trip had been for the funeral. But she hated it just as much.

"That's why," she said to Evie in a low voice. "That's why I don't like being here."

"Gwen! Evie!" The female voice echoed through the store, making Gwen wince. There was no flying under the radar in this town.

But when she turned and saw Molly Cyrs practically skipping down the aisle toward them, her mood brightened. Molly had that effect on people. With her dark hair pulled into a long ponytail that bounced as she moved and a grin that lit up her face, it was almost impossible not to feel instantly happier the second she entered a room. "Molly!"

After Mallory's lifelong best friend had hugged each of them, she stepped back and held up her hands. "I'd heard you were back and I was going to stop by sooner with a welcome-home pie, but you guys know I make the absolute worst pies, and my mom's been really busy and I didn't want to bring shame upon all future generations of my family by showing up with a store-bought pie, so...hey, welcome home!"

It was on the tip of Gwen's tongue to ask what was keeping Mrs. Cyrs—who loved to bake—so busy she couldn't make a pie, but she couldn't bring herself to ask the question. Molly's parents owned the Cyrs Funeral Home, so she wasn't sure she actually wanted to know why they were busy.

"We should have a girls' night out," Molly continued. "I mean, it won't be super fun until your bar opens because we don't actually have a bar yet, except at the restaurant, and the manager shushed me for laughing too loudly."

"That was at least six years ago," Gwen pointed out.

"There's no statute of limitations on trying to stifle my joy, Gwen." Molly sighed. "The important thing is that we get together before you two leave again."

"Definitely," Evie said. "And soon. There's no reason we can't have a little fun while we're in town, right, Gwen?"

Gwen thought of the manuscript still sitting unopened on her laptop and sighed. "No reason at all."

"And if you need help working on the carriage house, just let me know," Molly said. "I can usually sneak away for a while as long as nobody...well, you know."

"You might regret saying that when it comes time to paint all the walls," Evie said, and they both laughed. Gwen smiled, but she had a hard time mustering up their level of humor. She hated painting, and it was a reminder of just how long the list was of things they had to check off before she could get back to Vermont where she belonged.

By the time they'd spoken to several more people they ran into—thankfully none of whom seemed to care about *A Quaking of Aspens*—and bought the groceries they were after, Gwen was exhausted. She wasn't used to that much social interaction all at once, so after they'd gotten home and put everything away, she told Evie she was going for a walk.

She didn't, though. Instead, she went to the carriage house and made her way up the stairs. It felt a little like hiding, but she just wanted to chip away at a mindless task while she thought about her book on the off chance a scene would pop into her head. Sorting through decades of family debris cluttering the future office space would be perfect.

All she had to do was *not* think about Case.

* * *

Case wasn't even sure where to start. Despite his reassurances to the Sutton women that it wasn't so bad, the carriage house was in pretty rough shape. The actual brewing area in the cellar was perfection, of course, since that had been David's and Lane's priority, but they'd left the rest of it a mess.

The first thing they'd need was a worktable, he thought. Standing in the middle of the open space with a coffee in one hand and a clipboard in the other and no place to set them down wasn't ideal. The steps to what would eventually be the office seemed to be the only place to put them, so he walked over and dropped the clipboard onto a stair before taking a sip of the coffee. He probably should have brought an entire thermos if he wanted to get through this.

That's when he heard the noise upstairs.

Somebody was up there and he knew it wasn't Lane. Case had come straight over after work, but Lane had to do a few errands first. A glance over his shoulder told him Boomer had opted to stretch out on the granite step right outside the open door rather than join him inside, and he'd be content to stay there awhile, so Case started up the steps to see what was going on.

He wasn't sure who or what he'd expected to find, but it wasn't Gwen covered in grime and attacking the corner of the room with a broom. Apparently she was just moving boxes around and cleaning the floor for some reason. And she wasn't even using a good shop broom, but a regular kitchen model.

"It would probably be faster to use a Shop-Vac, you know," he said, and she whirled to face him, hand going to her chest.

After she'd glared at him and made some kind of growling sound that probably translated roughly to *don't you ever do that again*, she went back to sweeping. "I do know that, but I can't even hear myself think with one of those running. It's less about the cleaning and more about the mindless chores so I can think about plot and whatnot."

"So what's next in your plot?"

She threw him another hard glare. "If I knew, I wouldn't be covered in turn-of-the-century dust. And not the turn of the most recent century. The one before that."

When she reached for the dustpan, Case grabbed the half-full contractor bag to hold it open for her. The act of her dumping her sweepings into it kept putting their heads close together, and each time she leaned in close enough so he could smell her hair— a little bit of fruit under the ancient dust smell—he wanted to kiss her a little bit more.

When she was done, she brushed the wisps of hair that had escaped the ponytail from her smudged face. His fingers itched to do it for her. "Thank you."

"Anytime."

She tilted her head. "Why are you looking at me like that?"

If he kissed her, he was only going to make it worse. Rather than satisfying his craving for her, he knew a kiss would only whet his appetite for more. More kissing. More touching. More Gwen.

But he might as well be honest with her and get the telling of it out of the way, for better or worse. If she wasn't into him, things might be awkward for a while, but him staring at her mouth all the damn time wasn't any less awkward. "Because I'm obsessed with the thought of kissing you, and I'm not sure why."

Her cheeks reddened and she folded her arms across her chest, which only drew his attention to her breasts and did nothing to quell the urge to touch her. "That's so flattering and yet very much *not* at the same time."

"I've known you my entire life and, other than a brief time around middle school or so when I wanted to go to first base with literally every girl I laid eyes on, I never felt this way about you before. But now, there's just something about you and it won't let me be."

He could tell by the way her neck and cheeks flushed that she wasn't immune to the words, but she was shaking her head ever so slightly. "It doesn't matter because I can't date you, anyway. You're my sister's ex. That makes you off-limits to me."

Going out with Mallory had happened so long ago and was such a nonfactor, he laughed out loud. "You can't be serious."

"I didn't make the rule. It's just a rule. Girl code and all that."

"*Girl* being the important word there. Mallory and I were kids when we went out together. She and I have been friends for years. It's something *we* barely even think about anymore, but you're going to use it as an excuse to not want to kiss me?"

"It's not an excuse to *not* want to kiss you," she said, her cheeks even more pink now. "I *do* want to kiss you, actually. But it's the reason I'm not going to."

She wanted to kiss him. That was all he needed to hear because he wanted to kiss her and she wanted to kiss him and everything else was just noise. "Thinking about kissing you is costing me sleep, Gwen. I have a dangerous job."

She almost laughed, but he could see the softening in her expression. The way her lips parted. "That's not fair."

"Imagine it." He took a step closer and now she was within kissing distance. All she had to do was lean in and tip her head back. "Me, up in a tree, trying to cut a branch back from a power line, but all I can think about is how much I want to kiss you."

"I'd hate for you to get hurt," she said, and she sounded sincere, but the crinkling at the corners of her eyes and the lifted corners of her mouth gave away her amusement.

"I think my safety is more important than some silly rule from high school, don't you?" She couldn't really say no to that question, could she?

"No."

Dammit. He stepped back, holding up his hands in an *are you serious?* gesture. "No?"

"You seem to forget that I've known *you* for your entire life, Case Danforth, and one thing you're not going to do is slack on safety on the job. Do you think I've forgotten the hour-long safety demonstration and lecture you gave me when Dad wasn't around to show me how to use the electric hedge trimmer? An electric hedge trimmer, Case."

"Hey, you can really hurt yourself with one of those."

"You made me wear safety goggles. I was like fourteen. People saw me. I still kind of hate you for that." When she paused to take a breath, he knew she wasn't done. "And also, in keeping with the fact I know you, I also know you won't stop at a kiss. Next will be 'oh, Gwen, I can't safely run the chipper while I'm thinking about touching your boobs.'"

He laughed because she wasn't wrong, even though it did nothing to help his case. "I could touch your boobs *while* I kiss you, and then that won't be a problem."

When she pointed her finger at him, he knew he was doomed. "There are more bases, Case. And you'll want to round them all."

"No sense in playing the game if you're not looking to score." Then he winced. "I swear, you're turning me into a teenager again."

"And finally," she said, and she didn't look as

amused now. "It's not your safety versus a silly high school rule. It's about disrespecting my sister."

"I'm losing this debate badly, but I do want to point out that Mallory would rather have you kiss me than me fall out of a tree. She hasn't liked me *like that* in a lot of years, but she still likes me. And I haven't taught Jack how to run the snowblower yet."

Gwen narrowed her eyes. "Mal probably knows how to run the snowblower."

"Maybe, but she's so busy all the time. And your mom certainly shouldn't be doing it." He shrugged one shoulder, giving her a sheepish grin. "I hate to say it, but Mallory wouldn't want me falling out of a tree."

"You wear a safety harness."

A sigh of frustration escaped him before he could stop it. "Has anybody *ever* won an argument with you?"

She thought for a few seconds before frowning. "I guess Mallory has, because I told her I wasn't coming back to Stonefield, and yet here I am."

"Okay." It was time to try something else before she went too far down the path of remembering she was grumpy about being back in their hometown. "What if I call Mallory right now and ask her if she cares if I kiss you?"

Gwen's eyes widened. "You wouldn't dare."

He laughed and started reaching for his pocket. "A dare, Gwen?"

"No." Her hand grabbed his wrist before he could get his phone. "Not a dare. I did *not* mean that."

He noticed she hadn't let go of his wrist and he wasn't about to draw attention to the fact she was still touching him. "Because you know she won't care and you'll lose your excuse not to kiss me."

"I don't need an excuse. I can just say no."

"You absolutely *can* say no, and if you do, I won't bring it up again." He waited, giving her the opportunity to say it, but she neither said no nor let go of his wrist. "Or you can kiss me and we can both stop losing sleep wondering what it would feel like."

"Fine." When she tugged on his wrist and closed the gap between them, tilting her head back, he knew she was going to go about this in a Gwen kind of way—fast and to the point, and then she'd move on.

He wasn't going to let that happen. They were going to do this Case's way.

And Case's way was to slide one hand over her hip and with the other, he cupped the back of her neck. The first touch of his lips against hers was electric, and he felt the buzz throughout his entire body. She leaned in, her mouth softening under his, and he wished her hair was down so he could bury his fingers in it.

Taking his sweet time, he devoured her. Kissing her. Breathing with her. Dipping his tongue between her lips before catching her bottom lip gently between his teeth. Then deepening the kiss and demanding more. He never wanted the kiss to end, and judging by the way Gwen's body melted against his, she was okay with that.

Then her phone vibrated in her pocket and, with their bodies pressed together as they were, the sudden buzzing startled them both.

They were both breathing heavily and her cheeks were flushed a deep red as she took a step back. And he noticed her hands were shaking as she pulled out her phone, and when she made an annoyed sound and rolled her eyes, Case chuckled.

"Evie?"

She looked at him, the look of a woman who'd just been thoroughly kissed only slightly marred by the way her eyebrows drew together. "How did you know?"

"You made your *Evie* face. A little exasperation. Rolling of the eyes. Lips pressed together like you want to say something but won't." He didn't mention that it was extra cute because her lips were slightly puffy from him nibbling on them. "You're a lot more neutral when it's Mallory, and when it's Ellen, it's a much more affectionate exasperation than with Evie."

"Clearly you missed your calling as a professional poker player. So, Mr. Know-It-All, what face do I make when the text is from *you*?"

"I don't know because I'm not usually in the same room with you when I send a text. It's kind of the point." Pulling his phone out, he sent her a message, after making sure he wasn't accidentally sending it to the group's ongoing conversation.

See? This makes no sense.

Since she was looking at her phone—probably trying to read the message from Evie—he knew the instant the notification with his name on it popped up on the screen.

"Okay, so when it's me," he said, "your face gets a little flushed and you catch your bottom lip with your teeth, trying not to smile, but you can't help yourself."

She shot him a stern look. "Case."

"Hey, you asked."

"I have to go deal with Evie." She was between him and the stairs and backing away, so it didn't look like he was going to get a goodbye kiss. "You can't tell anybody about this."

"I wasn't going to take out an ad in the *Gazette*." He dipped his head into a little shrug. "They always need content for their Facebook page, though."

"This isn't funny, Case."

"I'm not going to tell anybody, Gwen."

"Okay, so we agree." She looked relieved. "It's not going to happen again, and we're not going to tell anybody. This never happened."

"Whoa." He held up one hand. "I didn't agree to all that. I said I wouldn't tell anybody. But I did kiss you. That definitely happened. And I'm going to kiss you again. It's pretty inevitable."

"Nothing's inevitable," she told him, but her gaze dropped to his mouth again before she turned and practically ran for the stairs, and he smiled.

Oh, it was inevitable, alright. He and Gwen weren't finished with the kissing yet. Not by a long shot.

Chapter Six

Don't miss the coupons from the Perkin' Up Café in this week's print issue! You can save money on fancy caffeinated beverages and breakfast foods, and they asked us to remind everybody you can also get a plain coffee and breakfast sandwich if that's what you're in the mood for. If you don't know the difference between a latte and a cappuccino, stop by the Perkin' Up Café! (And then message us because we don't know, either.)

—Stonefield Gazette *Facebook Page*

Saturday was the first day that Gwen opened her manuscript to find the words ready to flow, so of course Evie had to send a group text calling for a meeting after the thrift store closed at three o'clock. That would have been easy enough to bounce back from, as far as focus went, but it triggered an avalanche of text messages about everything from the topic of the meeting to the color the walls should be to how much a person would reasonably expect to pay for a plate of nachos.

Even those would have been easy to ignore until she was done with the writing for the day, but Case was a part of those conversations and seeing his name pop up on her phone gave her such a jolt of pleasure, she couldn't bring herself to set the phone to Do Not Disturb.

All she'd done since their kiss yesterday was think about kissing him again. If she *should* do it (no), and if she *wanted* to do it (yes) and when it could happen again (hopefully as soon as possible). Losing herself in her current story helped quiet that particular turmoil, which might be why she was finally getting some writing done, but every time she saw his name, the cycle started again.

She shouldn't have kissed him.

She shouldn't kiss him again.

She *wanted* to kiss him again and again and again.

While she'd never admit it, there had been a lot of pressure on that kiss because she'd been dreaming about Case kissing her for most of her life. She'd had a few actual relationships, of course. One that she even considered serious, though it had gone up in flames when he claimed she should have time to pick up his suit for a wedding they were attending because she did nothing but sit at a computer all day.

But when she closed her eyes and fantasized, it was always Case. And the man had not disappointed. The kiss they'd shared yesterday had been a long time coming, and totally worth the wait. Just remembering how his mouth had felt on hers and his hands on her body sent a frisson of desire down her spine, and she had to resist an urge to squirm in her chair.

She forced herself to reread the last few sentences she'd typed and then forced herself to focus enough to write a few more. And then she kept going.

By the time Eli pounded on her door and shouted that Aunt Evie wanted her to go downstairs, she'd written more over the course of the day than she had in the last month. Maybe mooning over her lifelong crush was good for the muse, she thought as she saved her work and closed the laptop. Or maybe it was being back in her old rocking chair. Either way, she was feeling good as she went down to join the others around the kitchen table. It probably would have made more sense to hold the meetings at the dining room table, but then they'd have no place to do puzzles.

She'd barely gotten through the kitchen door before her mom zeroed in on her. "I had four different people ask me today if I'm making sure you have a Sharpie, Gwen. What is that about?"

"I have no idea," she responded, frowning. She sat in the open chair, which happened to be across from Case. On the one hand, it was going to be hard not to spend the entire meeting looking at him. But on the other hand, she'd probably do it anyway, and this way she could look at him without getting a crick in her neck.

"I guess neither of you follows the *Stonefield Gazette* on Facebook," Mallory said with a chuckle.

"I certainly don't," Gwen said.

When her sister explained that the library was hoping to get some signed donations of *A Quaking of Aspens* for their Old Home Day book sale because they'd charge more for them, Gwen groaned. The entire town talking about her book again was the last thing she needed.

"They're raising money for the summer reading program, which your nephews do every year," Mal continued, "so I hope you'll be a good sport about it."

"Of course I will. I'm a good sport about signing books even if it doesn't benefit my nephews because I'm a professional. And I love libraries. Especially this one, and I always have." She'd spent a good amount of her childhood wandering the stacks, filling her tote with books to read and reread.

"I hate to draw attention away from Gwen's career," Evie said dryly, earning a sour look from Gwen. "But we really need to focus right now. If we finalize a name, I can still get some stuff printed in time for Old Home Day next weekend, even if it's just flyers printed off the computer. Just to get people excited."

They all turned to Lane, who looked a little uncomfortable with everybody suddenly staring at him. "The company name is Sutton-Thompson LLC, as you know. But we'd been talking about Sutton's Place for the brewery name. And the bar of course."

Nobody reacted right away. Gwen leaned back in her chair, running the name around in her head and trying to get a feel for how she liked it. She assumed everybody else was doing the same.

"Sutton's Place," Ellen said quietly, and her expression didn't offer any clues as to her reaction to it.

"When a property's been called something for years, it kind of sticks," Lane continued. "Heading to Sutton's place. Take a right after Sutton's place. Did you see the new stone wall at Sutton's place? It's what the house—and the carriage house—have been called for years. We were still kids when it went from being the old inn to being Sutton's Place."

"It doesn't include you, though," Ellen said. "Leaving you out of the name would have been bad enough when he was here, but now…it's *just* you."

Lane shook his head immediately. "It's not just me. It's half yours now. And without all of you, all I've got is too much beer to drink by myself. It still doesn't work without Suttons. And this might be a passion of mine, but it was David's dream."

Gwen wasn't the only one who had to blink back tears for a few seconds, but they needed to keep this moving forward. "Mom, does that bother you, with Sutton's Seconds and all?"

Ellen chuckled. "Sutton's Seconds. Sutton's Place. It's practically a Sutton empire."

They all laughed and then Evie held up her hand. "Do we vote? Or something? I want to nail this down so I can start getting the social media set up."

Their mom's eyes teared up again. "I like the idea of David's friends gathering at the Sutton's Place Tavern. When they get together and have a beer and relax, it'll be a little bit like they're with him, I think."

"Okay, but why *tavern*?" Evie asked.

"It sounds homey. Bar sounds so... I don't know, don't you think?" Ellen said.

Evie scowled. "How can I agree with what you don't know?"

"When I think of a bar, I think of a sports bar or a biker bar or something along those lines. Tavern sounds much warmer and welcoming."

"What about pub?" Mallory asked.

"Aren't pubs Irish?" their mother responded, and they all shook their heads. "Well, they seem Irish to me."

Lane cleared his throat. "Technically, it's a brewpub, since we brew the beer on-site. But, right or wrong, it doesn't sound like the kind of place a guy goes after a hard day at work to kick back with a cold one in this town."

"Tavern it is," Ellen declared, putting an end to the discussion. "Sutton's Place Brewery & Tavern."

Her eyes got a little misty then, and they all knew

she was thinking of her husband and how proud he would have been in this moment.

"To Sutton's Place Brewery & Tavern," Mal said, and she lifted her water bottle as if to make a toast.

"Wait! Hold that toast." Lane practically jumped out of his seat. "Everybody just stay here for a minute."

It was much longer than a minute, but Lane eventually returned, carrying a small glass bottle of amber liquid. "If we're going to toast to Sutton's Place, let's do it right."

Gwen didn't like beer, but this was a big moment, so she got up and pulled some plastic cups out of the sleeve they used for picnics. Lane poured a little bit in each cup before sitting down and lifting his in the air.

"To Sutton's Place," he said, and they all echoed the sentiment as they reached in to the center of the table to touch their plastic cups together.

There was no satisfying clink, but as Gwen lifted her cup to her mouth, she thought it was finer than any champagne toast she'd ever been a part of. Pain that her dad couldn't be here for this shot through her, but she rode it out and then refocused her attention on the happy faces around her, determined to live in the moment.

She *really* didn't like beer, though. Thankfully, she didn't grimace, though she noticed Mallory struggled to keep the smile going. She wasn't a beer drinker, either.

"This is actually good," Evie said, taking another sip, and Gwen watched her sister's gaze lock with Lane's over the rim of her cup.

"Thank you," he said, and relief washed over Gwen when the exes smiled at each other. Clearly Evie had been right and she just needed some time to process it. They'd be okay.

When Lane launched into an explanation of what kind of beer it was they were drinking and then went off into science, Gwen didn't exactly tune him out, but he didn't have her full attention, either. Case did. He was watching his cousin talk, occasionally nodding, and Gwen was looking at his profile.

She kept replaying that kiss in the carriage house over and over in her head. And remembering the way he'd looked at her before she'd walked away from him. The intense heat in his gaze had made a lot of promises that were probably best left broken.

Case wanted to do more than kiss her. Even though they were nothing alike and he knew she was essentially being held in Stonefield against her will, he still wanted her.

It didn't make sense. And neither did the fact she wanted him just as badly.

"Nothing like going from one meeting to another," Case said as he sank into his porch rocker and opened his laptop.

"That was a good meeting, though," Lane said, leaning his head back and smiling.

Case was happy for his cousin. The beer was good, the name was a go and next weekend they were going to officially let everybody in Stonefield know that there was going to be a new business in town. Word had already gotten out, of course. It was a small town. But now it officially had a name.

"It was a good one," he agreed. "But now we have to go over the pros and cons list we were each *supposed* to make for hiring another guy or two."

"I have a list," Lane said. "It's in my head."

"Doesn't do me a lot of good rattling around in there." The teasing was a long-standing thing because it was just how the two of them worked. Case liked to make notes and put thoughts on paper to analyze them. Lane mulled things over in his mind until he came to a conclusion. They'd been operating that way together for a long time and it worked.

They spent almost forty minutes going back and forth on the issue before they came to the conclusion that instead of hiring an expensive new foreman who'd be new to all of them, they'd promote their top guy and hire two greener guys. When it came to freeing up more time for the brewery, that was the smartest, most cost-effective way to do it in the long run.

"Maybe we should go sit in the backyard," Lane said, amusement heavy in his voice.

"Why would we do that? The folding camp chairs I stuck out there have nothing on these rockers."

"True, but you wouldn't be able to stare at the Sutton house instead of your laptop screen, hoping for a glimpse of Gwen."

Case felt his face get hot, so there probably wasn't any hope of laughing off his cousin's observation as all in his head. "I'm not staring at anything. I'm facing that direction, so if I look up from the computer, I'm looking at the house. That's it."

Maybe he'd looked up from his computer a lot more than usual since he sat down, but it was good for his neck to move those muscles. And they were getting done what they needed to. Where he looked was none of his cousin's business.

Lane laughed. "Sure. That must be it."

"I could turn my chair around and stare at the side of my house if it makes you feel like I'm being more productive."

Boomer lifted his head, maybe sensing some tenseness in Case's tone, but Lane just chuckled and reached down to stroke the dog's head. "It seems like I hit a nerve."

"You didn't *hit* a nerve. You're just *on* my last one."

"Okay. If you want to pretend I don't know you well enough to see what's going on, we can do that."

Lane had a point. There was probably nobody else on Earth who knew Case as well as his cousin did. There was enough of an age gap so they weren't super close as kids and they hadn't gone to school together, but as adults—especially since they worked together for the tree service their fathers had started—they'd become good friends and eventually, as close as brothers. He wasn't going to be able to keep secrets from Lane, no matter how much of an attitude Case threw his way.

"Fine," he snapped, earning a sharp look from Boomer. "I'm not sure how or why, but I seem to have developed a serious case of being hot for Gwen Sutton."

Lane kept his gloating to an *I knew it* smirk before shaking his head. "Hot for Gwen. I have to confess, that one *is* a little tough to figure out."

"It's a mystery," he said, though it really wasn't. For one, she was a great kisser, though he absolutely couldn't tell Lane how he knew that. He'd told Gwen he wouldn't.

"I mean, she's attractive."

Case nodded. "But bossy."

"Not really a people person," Lane added.

"She has a great laugh, though. And she's smart, and funnier than most people think she is. Even though she doesn't live here, she loves her family and she's here, helping them the best she can. She's great with Jack and Eli, and Boomer really seems to like her." When Lane didn't say anything for a few seconds, Case glanced over at his cousin to see him frowning slightly. "What?"

"I just… I don't know. I was expecting you to talk about how attractive she is and maybe make a comment about how she looks in tight jeans or something. But if you're talking about how she is with kids and how your dog likes her, maybe also keep in mind the part you said about her not living here. And remind yourself that she's going back to Vermont as soon as she gets the chance. She hates it here."

"I'm not ring shopping or anything."

"You also don't sound like a man laying out his reasons for wanting a quick hookup with a woman."

Maybe because he didn't want a quick hookup. He already knew that wouldn't be enough to get Gwen Sutton out of his system. Yes, he knew she had no interest in spending any more time in Stonefield than she had to, but maybe she just hadn't had the right incentive to stay.

"Nope." Lane was shaking his head. "Don't do that."

"Don't do what?"

"You're wondering if you can be enough to make her want to stay."

Case frowned. Being like brothers was one thing. Lane being able to read his mind was quite another. He shook his head, because he wanted to dismiss his cousin's words, but he didn't want to verbalize an outright lie and deny it.

"Trust me," Lane continued. "If a woman doesn't want to settle down here, you can't make her. She'd just be unhappy anyway, and eventually it would all fall apart."

Case didn't say anything right away because he knew this wasn't just about Gwen anymore. Lane and Evie had planned to leave Stonefield and travel after

they got married. Maybe they'd return to town to settle down or maybe they'd find someplace they'd like
better, but they were going to see what was out there.

Then Lane's dad had passed away and Lane was
left with a mother who was not only grieving, but
drew her income from helping out D&T Tree Service by manning the phone and doing paperwork.
Case's dad would never have left his sister-in-law
to fend for herself, but Lane wasn't one to shirk responsibility, so he took over his father's place in the
company. Months passed and they settled into a life
that Evie hadn't chosen for herself—a life she didn't
want. She left Stonefield without him.

Lane definitely had good reason to believe a man
who intended to stay in his hometown getting involved with a woman who wanted to leave it was a
really bad idea.

Case would just have to keep his expectations in
check. Yes, he'd been increasingly aware over the last
several years that he'd really like to meet a woman
who he'd want to spend the rest of his life with, but
that didn't mean he couldn't have a fling while he
waited. There had to be a woman out there he'd want
as much as he wanted Gwen Sutton.

Maybe. Somewhere.

And then she stepped out onto the porch of the
Sutton house, and suddenly it didn't seem at all likely
there was another woman out there who'd have her
effect on his heart rate.

Gwen glanced over at them and she was too far

away for eye contact, but he knew she was looking at him. After a few seconds, she waved, and then she went down the steps and started toward the carriage house. He was content to watch her walk until his cousin's voice ruined the moment.

"I can't wait to hear what excuse you're going to come up with for having an urgent need to go over to the carriage house and talk to her."

He'd actually been trying to come up with one, but there was no way he'd admit that to Lane. "You're just hoping to get out of the rest of this meeting, and that's not going to happen."

Though he managed to get through the rest of the information they needed to go over and finalize their schedule for the following week, he kept those neck muscles nice and limber by looking up from his laptop very frequently.

Fifteen minutes after she went to the carriage house, Gwen left it and walked back to the main house. She did glance over and give a little wave, but then she disappeared inside and he found himself wondering what she'd gone to the carriage house for. Was she checking on something? Getting a measurement?

Or had she been hoping he'd see her and join her there? Right now, short of her walking across the street and into his house, it was the only place they could be alone. And he didn't think Gwen was resigned enough to the inevitability of their kissing again to show up on his doorstep.

"You know," Lane said, "when you said things were about to get interesting the night Gwen and Evie got back to town, I thought you meant because of Evie and me."

"I did."

"Maybe you did at the time, but I have a feeling you and Gwen are going to be a *lot* more interesting than me and my ex-wife."

Case couldn't hold back the grin as he looked over at his cousin. "I certainly hope so."

Chapter Seven

With regard to donating books to the library's
Old Home Day sale, please note they will not
accept books that would have been discarded
from their collection before you were born.
For instance, if a parenting how-to book says
it's perfectly fine to shove six kids in the back
of a station wagon, you should probably throw
it away.

—Stonefield Gazette *Facebook Page*

Gwen parked as close to the front door of Sutton's
Seconds as she could get, so she wouldn't have to
walk down the main street and get accused of doing
who-knew-what to who-knew-who in her books. She
would rather have been in her rocking chair, work-

ing on her *next* book, but one did not ignore a text message from one's mother. Her visit today was by order of maternal command.

Some of her annoyance at being summoned dissipated as she looked up at the Sutton's Seconds sign over the door and massive window. Behind the glass was a summer display, filled with items people would want as the kids started their break.

She'd spent so much time here growing up, it was almost an extension of *home* in her mind. There was a room in the back that served for sorting and pricing items, or for stashing things that needed cleaning or repair. But it also had a small table and chairs, and back in the day, a futon. She wasn't sure if the futon was still there, but she had clear memories of being tucked in on it with a blanket and some books when she was too sick to go to school, but not sick enough for her mom to close the shop for the day.

All three of the girls had worked there—starting in middle school since the labor laws didn't really apply to your own kids—until they got old enough to find jobs that didn't include their mother being their boss. Working in Sutton's Seconds had been Gwen's favorite job, though. It wasn't exactly demanding work, so she'd had plenty of time to daydream and make up stories in her head. Eventually she'd started scribbling those stories in cheap spiral notebooks. Now she had a custom journal cover with her name embossed in the leather—bought because the leather looked and smelled like her father's journal—but stepping through the thrift store doors made her feel like that story-loving girl again, and she smiled. This was where her career had been born.

Maybe she should bring her laptop here and hide at the table in the back room and see if that helped her get words on the screen. The words had been flowing, but then the urgency of the logo situation had proven to be an interruption—or series of interruptions, really—that she couldn't bounce back from.

In order to have a finished logo in time to show it off at Old Home Day, they needed to rush a concept to the designer who did most of the graphics for Gwen's book promotion. Lane had texted them a page from her father's journal, and seeing her dad's handwriting had really taken a toll on her creativity. Then there was a lengthy text chain while they decided which of the three concepts the designer sent best brought David's logo to life.

Now it was official. The words *Sutton's Place Brewery & Tavern* against the backdrop of a field with three lupines—one of Ellen's favorite flowers for each of his daughters. But it had been a lot, both emotionally and in terms of time, and the words had dried up.

"Gwen!" Ellen's face lit up with joy when she saw her. "Mallory, your sister's here."

Her sister emerged from the children's clothing section, not as thrilled to see her as their mom had been, but at least she was smiling. "Oh good, you're here. We've gotten two more copies in since Mom messaged you."

And that's when Gwen saw the stacks of books on the counter. All three of her books were represented, but *A Quaking of Aspens* definitely dominated the piles. "Why are these here?"

"Rather than having people trying to chase you down individually or putting extra work on the library staff, Mom put the word out that donations of your book could be dropped off here and you'd sign them all."

"So here's a question," Gwen said, staring at the books. "If everybody donated their copies to the sale, who's going to buy copies *from* the sale?"

Mallory laughed. "Anybody who wants a signed copy, I guess. But I did tell the librarian to pull any signed copies that don't sell and give them to me. I'll sell them online and split the money with the summer reading program. Get to signing."

Gwen was going to point out she usually didn't sign books with a Sharpie and had a special gel pen she preferred to use, but she didn't think that particular fact would endear her to her sister at all. "Fine, but I'm using the bathroom first."

She didn't take long since she wanted to get this over with as soon as possible and get back to her book, but when she stepped out of the bathroom, she almost collided with Case.

"What are *you* doing here?" she asked, and then— when he took a step back and frowned slightly—she immediately regretted the question. And the unnecessarily harsh way she'd asked it. "I'm sorry. I was just surprised to see you. I guess you're here for the same reason everybody else comes here."

"Probably not."

"No?" It was her turn to frown, even as she did her best to look anywhere but at his mouth. That wasn't easy since all she seemed to do anymore was think about kissing him again.

"Not unless everybody else comes here because they saw your car parked outside and thought it might be a good time to stop in and see if your mom has anything we can snag to use for some kind of Old Home Day booth." He grinned. "I get to see you and possibly find a folding table at the same time. I'm efficient that way."

"You see me every day," she pointed out, but she could feel her cheeks flush. She liked that he wanted to see her, even if it did nothing to cool that ember of desire that would be better off doused in cold water. "The outdoor stuff's in the back."

"You're not going to help me shop?"

"I don't work here," she reminded him. "You already know where everything is, and I have to sign books for the library sale."

Then she walked away before he could talk her into it. She had a hard time resisting him, but the last thing she wanted to do was have her mother and sister watching the two of them together—especially after her mom saw her checking out his butt the other day. It would put ideas in their heads, and she was having a hard enough time dealing with the ideas Case put in her *own* head. She absolutely did not want either of her sisters, but especially Mallory, to guess how she felt about Case. Or find out they'd been kissing in the carriage house.

Gwen signed the stack of books faster than she'd ever signed books before and then, after promising her mother she'd come in again if they took in any more, she drove back to the house so she could get more words in before everybody gathered for dinner.

She didn't see Case again until she got up to find the end of the cord so she could plug her laptop back in and movement in the window caught her eye. Movement in *his* window.

His bedroom window, to be precise.

As she watched, unable to tear her gaze away, he peeled off the hooded D&T Tree Service T-shirt he'd been wearing at the thrift store and flung it. Even if he had a bigger window, she wouldn't have seen where it landed because she couldn't look away from his broad chest and taut abs. Hard work definitely did a body good.

She could only see him from the waist up, but when his arms made a downward pushing motion and then he bent over, she realized he was taking off his pants. A squeaky sound escaped her lips and she spun around so her back was to the window. What was *wrong* with her?

With deliberate concentration, she found the end

of her charger cord and plugged it into the port on her laptop before carefully setting the computer on the table next to her rocker. But before she stepped away, she couldn't resist just one more quick peek out the window.

For a few seconds she thought he'd pulled a blind down and he was a little late with that, but then she realized she was looking at a big piece of cardboard with words printed across it.

He'd written the words so large, she didn't even have to squint to read them.

Hi peeping Gwen.

Her cheeks flamed and she jerked away from the window, hoping he wasn't watching to see her reaction.

Peeping Gwen?

No way was she letting that stand. She could look out her window whenever she wanted. If a person was planning to strip, that person bore the responsibility of closing his damn curtains and giving himself privacy.

She hurried down the stairs and into the kitchen, where she found Mallory pulling a lasagna out of the oven and didn't manage a U-turn before her sister saw her.

"Oh, Gwen. Want to start setting the table?"

"Definitely, but I need like five minutes first. That has to sit before you can cut it anyway, right?" Mal frowned, but this was too important to wait until *after* dinner. "Do you have any poster board kicking around? Like from the boys' science fair projects or something?"

Mallory frowned. "I'm not sure. Why do you need poster board?"

Even though she should have seen the question coming, she didn't have an answer for that. Not one that she cared to share, anyway. "It's for…my book. Yeah, for writing. I like to put notes up on poster board sometimes so I can see them."

"There might be some in the shop room. Sometimes Mom uses it to make signs for the store, so if we have any, that's where it would be. Jack and Eli haven't really hit science fairs yet, though I know it won't be long before there are last-minute poster board and wine runs in my future."

"Thanks." Going back up the stairs—at least being home was good exercise—she went to the small room next to the master suite.

It was a weird space, too small to be a bedroom, but too big to be a closet. Gwen had vague memories of clunky shelves in the back of it, and they assumed it had been a monster linen closet during the house's time as an inn. Her dad had installed modular shelving at some point, so it had new shelves and a few drawers, along with a clothing rack down one side. A small table with a stool were centered in the middle, and her mom used it as a place to store and prep items for the thrift shop that were dropped off with her at the house, or that the family was looking to get rid of.

Much to her delight, she didn't find poster board,

but she found a whiteboard that would be even better. In a plastic bag taped to the back of it, she found a fat black dry erase marker and an eraser, so she had everything she needed. She'd have to remember to stick an IOU in its place—which they were all supposed to do if they took something from the shop room—but for now she turned off the light and took the whiteboard back to her room.

He shouldn't have embarrassed her. Case thought about the sign he'd put in his bedroom window the entire time he was cooking his dinner, and around the time he dumped the pasta from the strainer to his plate, it hit him that Gwen might not take the friendly ribbing in the way he'd intended. It was teasing. A joke. She had to know that.

But what if she didn't? Or maybe she saw the joke, but didn't find it funny. He should remove it and hope she hadn't seen it. He should also remember to close his curtains before he stripped down to take a shower.

Leaving the plate of pasta on the counter, he took the stairs at a jog, Boomer on his heels. The Suttons were probably eating *their* supper, he told himself. There was a good chance they were all gathered together in the kitchen and she hadn't seen the sign yet.

But when he yanked the cardboard out of his window, a glance across the street told him he was too late. There appeared to be a large whiteboard in Gwen's window and he had to squint a little, but he could read the block letters she'd used to write her response.

I'll throw you a dollar, but I want a quarter back.

It took a few seconds for her meaning to sink in, and then he laughed so suddenly he startled the dog. Boomer gave him a quizzical look that made him laugh harder.

He was going to have to up his teasing game, because not only did Gwen Sutton definitely have a good sense of humor, but she had a bit of a mean streak, as well. He liked that about her. He liked it so much, as a matter of fact, he smiled the entire time he ate his spaghetti, even though the pasta had gotten clumpy while he was upstairs because he hadn't put the sauce on it yet.

Case wouldn't have thought anything could distract him from goopy noodles, but apparently he liked thinking about Gwen Sutton that much.

She even kept him company—mentally, anyway— while he cleaned up after supper and threw a load of dirty clothes into the washer, including the ones he'd just stripped off in clear view of the woman's window.

It had been an accident on his part. He'd been working with an exceptionally sap-covered stand of trees and if he didn't get those clothes off, every strand of dog hair in the place—and Boomer was a shedder—was going to be plastered to him. And he might stick to his furniture.

He just wanted out of the clothes, and he hadn't given any thought to dropping the blind. And Gwen had slept in that room so seldom over the years, it never crossed his mind she might be standing in her window, looking through his. But then—through the corner of his eye, so she might not have even realized he'd seen her—he caught her watching him.

He'd been in the process of dropping his pants, so there wasn't a lot he could do about it in that moment. By the time he'd gotten the jeans to his ankles, ready to kick them off, another quick glance told him she'd disappeared, which was a relief. He hadn't been sure how much she'd be able to see above his windowsill if he stood up again. After yanking the jeans back up, he went to close the blind, but then he got the idea of making the sign just to tease her a little.

Boomer made a woofing sound that caught his attention, jerking him out of his thoughts of Gwen. The dog was standing on the couch, his front legs on the back of it so he could see out the window.

"You're not supposed to do that," Case reminded the dog as he knelt next to him so he could see who was out there. Definitely not a squirrel, since Boomer's squirrel bark was much higher pitched and tended to include some half-ass attempts at howling. "Who's out there?"

It was Gwen. Not coming up his sidewalk, naked under a trench coat, unfortunately. But she was walking from the Suttons' porch toward the carriage house, and Boomer woofed again.

"You want to go see Gwen?" Case asked, and the dog was off the couch and sprinting to the door.

Case didn't move quite as fast, but he felt the same as Boomer on the inside.

Gotta go see Gwen!

By the time they crossed the street, she was already inside the carriage house, and he tried to manage his expectations. For all he knew, Gwen was joining her family and he'd walk through the door only to find all four Sutton women inside. While his goal was to sneak a few minutes alone with her, he didn't want to get his hopes up too much. Well, any higher than they already were, at least. He'd been hoping to kiss her again since the first time he kissed her.

He breathed a sigh of relief when he stepped inside the building and found Gwen alone. Or maybe the sigh was his breath leaving his body at the sight of her on her hands and knees, looking under the worktable for...something. The yoga pants she was wearing hugged her butt in a way that made his own clothes feel too tight below the waist.

Boomer bounded over to see why she wasn't standing on her two legs like people usually did, and luckily his tags jingled, so she knew he was coming. Case would have felt bad if they'd startled her into smacking her head on the underside of the worktable.

"Boomer!" She backed out from the under the table and stood, brushing off her knees. Then she gave his fur a good tousle, causing his wagging tail to become a joyful blur.

"Did you lose something under there?" Case asked as she greeted his dog.

"We're on a hunt for Jack's left earbud. He was out here earlier, so I volunteered to check since it was better than listening to everybody yell at him, asking where he'd left it, and him yelling back that if he knew that, it wouldn't be lost."

"He's not wrong." He noticed she was looking everywhere but directly at him, and her cheeks were slightly flushed. Maybe it was from crawling around on the floor, or maybe it was because he'd caught her watching him take his clothes off. "Did you bring my dollar?"

Throwing it out there so directly made her flush darken, and she gave him an arch look, but at least she was looking at him now. "Did you bring a quarter?"

He patted where his pockets would be if he was wearing jeans, but he'd thrown on a pair of gray sweatpants and a T-shirt after his shower. "Damn. Left it in my other pants."

In his peripheral vision, he noticed Boomer was wandering off to sniff around the floor, but most of his attention was on Gwen. Somehow the gap had closed between them—as if they simply gravitated toward each other—and she was close enough to touch now.

And he did. Rather than reach out and grab her and pull her close, despite feeling a strong urge to do just that, he trailed his fingertips down her arm. It gave her plenty of opportunity to back away, but she didn't. When his fingers reached her wrist, he circled it and gave a gentle tug.

She let him pull her close enough to kiss, her head tipping back as her gaze locked onto his mouth. He released her wrist in anticipation of having both hands free to roam her body as he kissed her senseless. "I told myself I wasn't going to kiss you again."

"I'm glad you don't write nonfiction, then," he said, and she rolled her eyes, but her lips curved into a smile. "But I'm not sure I want to kiss you after you implied my stripping talents were subpar."

"In my defense, I could only see you from the waist up. There may have been some hip action I missed."

He laughed despite his cheeks suddenly feeling hot. "There was no hip action."

Her eyebrow arched. "Well, if you don't want to kiss me, I'll just go inside and—"

She turned as though to walk away, and he panicked. His hand shot out and circled her wrist again, tugging her back to him. But in his desire to keep her there, he tugged a little harder than he intended to, pulling her up so hard against his body that he had to take a step back to brace himself against the impact.

Gwen laughed that laugh he loved so much, and her eyes were crinkled in amusement as she tipped her head back.

His breath caught in his throat. This was the picture of Gwen he wanted branded into his memory forever—the Gwen he liked to think nobody else got to see. With her hair tousled and her eyes sparkling with humor. The rosy flush over her cheeks at whatever she saw in his eyes when their gazes locked. Her lips parting slightly as she anticipated his mouth lowering to hers.

This was *his* Gwen.

A sudden fear that she would see in his eyes what he was feeling spurred him to close the distance— his eyes closing as his lips met hers.

Her body melted against his, and he ran his hands up her hips and her back before he wrapped his arms around her. One of her hands gripped his shoulder and the other slid up his chest to cup his jaw, and he had to bite back a moan as he deepened the kiss.

Gwen returned his kiss with a passion that made his blood heat, and he slid one hand under the hem of her shirt so he could feel the hot, smooth flesh of her back. He stroked her skin, slowly working his way up until his fingertips hit the strap of her bra.

The thought of undoing that clasp and sliding his hand under the fabric to cup her breast made his entire body quiver with anticipation, and he caught her lower lip between his teeth for a moment before sliding his tongue over the same spot.

Before he could attempt to undo the clasp one-handed, though, Gwen braced her hands against his shoulders and gently pushed against them.

He obliged, taking a step back, as they both tried to catch their breath. Her eyes reflected the same heat that was currently burning him up, but common sense returned along with his ability to breathe, and he admitted to himself that the dirty cement floor of a half-done tavern was not the place to make his nocturnal dreams of Gwen come true.

"This is not…" She paused, then waved her hand in a way that encompassed the carriage house. And she was back to looking anywhere but at him. "This isn't a good idea."

He wasn't sure exactly what she meant was a bad idea—kissing him where anybody could walk in on them, kissing him in a carriage house deep in the throes of renovation, or just kissing him at all. He really hoped it wasn't the latter. "I know I want to keep kissing you, Gwen, and I'm pretty sure you want to keep being kissed."

"No!" she exclaimed, and his stomach dropped. That was a pretty emphatic *no*. "What's in Boomer's mouth?"

Case would have been more relieved that her shouted *no* had been for the dog and not him, but concern for Boomer trumped everything and he gave the command on instinct. "Drop it."

Boomer tilted his head, staring at him. *Drop what?*

"Please tell me he didn't eat Jack's earbud," Gwen said with a sigh.

"I don't know. Maybe we could have Jack play his music and see if Boomer's stomach sings to us." He was walking toward his dog as he said it, and she didn't respond, so he didn't know if she'd found the suggestion amusing or *not funny* at all.

Boomer reluctantly let Case unlock his jaws, but there was nothing in his mouth. When he looked around the floor, though, he noticed that the dog was refusing to move and was avoiding eye contact as if the most interesting thing Boomer had ever seen was on the wall to their right.

After nudging the dog's butt until he had to shift his weight or fall over, Case pulled out the small plastic bag containing a few kernels of popcorn that Boomer had been trying to hide from him by sitting on it. "Popcorn."

The relief was evident on Gwen's face. "I guess Eli's been out here, too, since that kid never goes anywhere without a bag of popcorn. I'm so glad it wasn't Jack's earbud. I wouldn't put it past Mallory to make one of us watch Boomer at all times until he…gave the earbud back, so to speak."

"You could have volunteered," he said, and then he winced. "I mean, not so much for monitoring the return of the earbud, but for being with Boomer 24/7."

"As delightful as he is, why would I volunteer to spend 24/7 with your dog?"

"Because my dog spends 24/7 with *me*."

Just as understanding of what he was getting at made her eyebrow arch, they were interrupted by Jack bursting through the door, yelling for his aunt Gwen. "We found it—it was in the freezer with the popsicles—and Mom said I should tell you so you can come back in the house."

Case didn't want Gwen to go back in the house. He didn't want her to walk away until they'd come to some kind of understanding about what was happening between them. That would involve him telling her all of the things he'd like to have happen—most of which involved not so much as a layer of cotton between them—and her telling him whether she'd like to have those things happen, as well. It wasn't exactly a conversation they could have while her ten-year-old nephew was standing right there, feeding the remnants of Eli's popcorn to Boomer.

And when their eyes met over the boy and dog, the desire to escape such a conversation was written all over her face. Maybe she'd caught his *we need to talk* vibe or maybe she just knew it was time they figure out and put words to what they were doing, but she obviously wanted no part of it.

"Better it fell into the freezer drawer than the toilet, I guess," Gwen said, and Case was dismayed to see she was already moving toward the door. There was no doubt she was going to take advantage of Jack's interruption to make her escape. "You don't mind closing everything up, do you, Case?"

"Of course not." He gave her a benign smile for Jack's benefit, but tried to let her know with a slight narrowing of his eyes that he was on to her and they *would* be revisiting the kissing issue.

And it would be soon.

Chapter Eight

Found: a cell phone in the vicinity of the gas station and turned in to the police station. It's locked, but there is a photo of a celebrity with a rather foulmouthed quote on the lock screen. To claim it, stop at the police station and identify the celebrity and quote. (Hint: it's not our own Gwen Sutton, though she certainly does like to use obscenities in her books.) Margaret at the front desk has requested you not actually use the four-letter word in the quote, or she will submerge your phone in hot, soapy water.
— Stonefield Gazette *Facebook Page*

There was something worse than waking up to two boys yelling about whose turn it was to do a chore and their mother yelling at them to figure it out and their grandmother yelling at everybody to stop yelling.

That was waking up to an email from her agent.

Of course he opened with hoping the email found her well. She wasn't so sure about that part. Then came the dreaded phrase "no pressure, *but*," followed by the reassurance he just wanted to check in and see how the writing was going, and see if there was anything he could do to help.

The translation of course, was that her deadline was approaching faster than either of them would like and she'd already been given an extension. She'd had a valid reason for that, seeing as her father had passed away. Being sucked into trying to open a bar and spending all of her free time daydreaming about kissing the grown version of her teen crush again weren't quite as good, as excuses went.

After assuring him it was going really well— she did write fiction, after all—she took a shower, made her bed and did a few other things until the house was quiet. Once she was fairly certain everybody was either gone or busy doing something anywhere but in the room with the coffee maker, she went downstairs.

She'd been wrong. Mallory was still in the kitchen, sitting at the table with a notepad in front of her. From a brief glance as she passed by on her way to the coffee, Gwen thought it was a grocery list, but she wasn't sure. "Good morning."

"'Morning," Mallory replied without looking up from the notepad.

"Grocery list?" After fixing her coffee, she sat down and took a sip. Half-and-half definitely needed to be on that list if that's what her sister was doing, because it was already getting low and she absolutely didn't want to go without again.

"Sort of." Mallory set down her pen and took a sip of her own coffee. "Mom wants to try a few recipes out for the bar, so I'm making an ingredients list so we can experiment with the menu."

Gwen's eyes widened. "Are we at that point already?"

Her sister shrugged. "Not really, but we don't want to wait until the last minute. And Mom can't really help with the construction, so working on this gives her a way to feel like she's doing something."

When Mallory picked up her pen and went back to her list, her attention bouncing between the notepad and whatever was on her tablet's screen, Gwen sat back and drank her coffee, content to let the conversation lapse.

Without talking about the brewery to distract her, though, her mind wandered to Case. It always did if she didn't have something specific to think about, but thinking about him—constantly reliving their kisses over and over—while sitting across from Mallory made her uncomfortable.

She felt guilty. Guilty for kissing her sister's ex-boyfriend. Guilty for hiding it. Guilty for wanting to kiss him again.

"What is going on, Gwen? You keep looking at me like you want to tell me something, but also *don't* want to tell me something, and I have too much going on in my life to guess what it is."

Gwen drew in a deep breath and then decided it was best to get it over with. "I kissed Case."

"You *what*?"

"Twice."

"Twice?"

"But I'm not going to date him," Gwen continued in a rush. "It was just a couple of kisses and I'm sorry."

Mallory was clearly confused. "You kissed Case? And you're sorry about what? I feel like you're giving me random puzzle pieces here."

"He's your ex," Gwen said. "You're not supposed to date your sister's ex."

"We dated in high school. That was a long time ago."

"They say you never forget your first."

"Of course I can't forget my first. He lives across the street." After a few seconds, Mallory laughed so suddenly it startled Gwen. "Is that what's going on here? Seriously, Gwen?"

"What?"

"You won't go out with Case because I dated him when we were teenagers?" When Gwen didn't say anything, she laughed again. "You've got to be kidding me."

Gwen didn't think the conversation was all that funny. "Everybody knows your sisters' exes are off-limits. That's a thing."

"It's so not a thing." It actually was, so Gwen just waited her sister out. "Okay, it's kind of a thing, but not in this case. No, you couldn't have gone with Case to, like, senior prom or anything after we broke up. But it's been *years*, Gwen. A lot of years. I've been married. Had two kids. Divorced. I don't live in high school anymore. Neither does he."

"I find it hard to believe it wouldn't be weird for anybody."

"It honestly wouldn't." Mallory held up her hands. "Look, he's almost like a brother to me. I say *almost* because the fact remains we did actually date all those years ago, and that would make it weird."

Gwen chuckled, but she got the point. "So you wouldn't care if I went out with Case, then?"

"I…" Her sister let that reply die away, looking decidedly uncomfortable. "I don't think you should *not* go out with Case because I dated him in high school."

"So what's your real reason for why I shouldn't go out with him?" Gwen pushed, because it was clear Mal had reservations.

"This is none of my business."

"Like that's ever stopped anybody in this family. Or in this town, for that matter. Just tell me."

Mallory inhaled deeply before blowing out a

sharp breath. "Fine. I think you'll hurt him, and I don't want that to happen because he's a really good friend."

Gwen sat back in her seat, eyes wide. "I'll hurt *him*?"

She didn't want to get into the history of the situation brewing between her and Case. The fact that she'd had a crush on him forever and he'd been interested in her for like five minutes meant that, of the two, Gwen was far more likely to be the one who walked away with a broken heart. Mallory didn't need to know just how long she'd been dreaming of kissing him, though.

Maybe it would be silly if her attraction to Case was new. They were adults now and high school had been a long time ago. But Gwen had wanted Mallory's ex since before he was even her sister's boyfriend—and during and after—so that guilt was baked into her feelings about him at this point.

"Case is here a lot," Mallory continued. "I know him really well, and he's at a point in his life where he's thinking about having a family. He needs to date women who might be the one, so he can get married and have kids. You're not staying, Gwen. You've made it very clear you're leaving the first minute you can without *too* much guilt, and that's not fair to him."

Gwen had gone into this conversation talking about hooking up, not marriage and babies. "Nobody's planning a wedding, Mal. But for the sake of argument, he could move to Vermont. It's not that different from New Hampshire, you know."

Mallory snorted. "Except that his family and friends are all here. And the house he owns. And the business he owns. This is where his life is. And believe it or not, some people *like* Stonefield and actually choose to live here."

Gwen stood and picked up her notebook. "This is just becoming another condemnation of me *choosing* to live in Vermont, and I'm not interested."

"It's really not," Mal said quietly. "It's the truth. You don't want to stay here, and Case doesn't want to leave. If we were all twenty years old, it wouldn't be a big deal. Have a fun fling. But I'm just saying, that's not where Case is in his life, so if you decide to go for it, just make sure you're both on the same page. I wouldn't know, since I have no clue what page *you're* ever on."

"I'm definitely not on any page that has me spending the rest of my life in this town."

"You never really talk about your personal life, you know. Just how the writing's going and stuff like that."

There was no admonishment in her sister's tone. Gwen only heard a touch of sadness, which compelled her to be honest. "That is my personal life, Mal. I don't really get out and meet people. There was one guy I saw a couple of times, but then Dad died and… that guy wasn't my person. I don't have one. Just the writing."

Mallory gave her a small smile. "I get it. I don't have a person, either. Just the kids. But the question here is if you're *looking* for a person and if that person could be Case because, like I said, same page and all that."

Gwen opened her mouth to tell her sister she and Case were on the same page, but then she shut it again because she actually didn't know if that was true. She didn't even know what page *she* was on, never mind Case.

They'd kissed. She'd watched him undress, though only from the waist up, through his bedroom window and then implied his stripping skills were lacking. Then they'd kissed again. That didn't mean they were in an actual relationship or that either of them even wanted to be.

She certainly didn't. For her, it was simply a matter of being attracted to a man for so long that she was powerless to resist him now that he'd finally noticed her. And she still hoped to be out of there by the end of the summer. There was no page to be on because there was no book. It was a short story. A vignette.

It was just a slice of life. A small but dreamy and delicious slice.

Case's phone buzzed in his pocket for what felt like the hundredth time that morning, but he ignored it until the bucket he was strapped into had been lowered to the ground and he could unhook himself. The hydraulic arm wasn't fast, but he was able to answer it before it went to voice mail.

It was Lane's mom, Laura, who still answered the business phone for them. "Toby Smart just called because his cat is stuck up in a tree."

He snorted. "Did you tell him that cutting the tree down seems like a pretty radical way to get a cat out of it?"

"He asked that you bring the truck over and use the bucket to rescue Evangeline."

"Evangeline? Did a woman go up after the cat?"

"No, that's the cat's name." Laura sighed. "Since it was shared with me at length, would you like to hear the story of how Toby rescued a kitten named Cuddles from the shelter, but decided to rename her something grand so she could aspire to great things?"

"Like getting stuck in a tree?" He scrubbed his hand over his sweaty, grimy-feeling face, thinking about the shower that was practically calling his name. "He should call the fire department."

"They told him to put food out and when the cat is hungry, she'll come down. He tried that around noontime, but Evangeline wasn't interested and his neighbor gave him a lengthy lecture about how every squirrel and skunk in town was going to show up on their street."

"I'm wrapping up this job, and his place is between here and Lane's, so I'll stop by. If the cat's still in the tree, I'll see what I can do."

"I'll call him back. Since Toby gave it to me, do

you want to hear the list of Evangeline's likes and dislikes as to being touched and spoken to so this can be as nontraumatic as possible for his sweet angel?"

His growl made Laura laugh, and she was still laughing when he hung up on her.

An hour later, a very irate Evangeline had been reunited with her owner on the ground, and Case bore a few battle wounds on his hands and neck. They burned like fire thanks to his being allergic to cats, and he thought about that shower waiting for him again while Toby secured Evangeline in the house and paid him for the call. What Case was charging him was barely worth the time it took to write the check, but their fathers had learned soon after starting the tree service that owning equipment that could reach higher than the average ladder meant they'd spend a good chunk of their time doing "quick favors" for people if they didn't draw a line. The Danforths and Thompsons didn't mind helping out their neighbors from time to time, but if the truck was required, a check needed to be written.

The crew—who'd left the job in the truck pulling the chipper—had already gone home when he arrived at his cousin's house, so he parked the boom truck in the row with the other equipment and started his personal truck to let the AC run. Boomer had left with Lane earlier in the day since it was hot and they were cutting down the only shade tree in the customer's yard, so after running the two checks in to Laura—who forced him to submit to having his

cat scratches cleaned and lathered with ointment—
he was free to head for home.

When he pulled into his driveway, Boomer didn't
run to the sidewalk and bark, waiting for the signal
to cross as he usually did after Jack and Eli wore him
out and he was ready to come home. Lane's truck and
all of the Sutton vehicles were in the driveway, which
meant they were probably in the carriage house.

He should go over and see what they were up to.
See if there was anything he could do to help. But
he was hot and grubby and exhausted, and—if he
was being honest with himself—a little resentful that
Lane had taken off early. Case knew there would be
more and more of that the closer they got to opening the brewery, and he was mostly okay with it,
but there were times he'd like to be the one hanging
out in a climate-controlled glass room brewing beer.

Case stayed in the shower until the water ran cold,
and then threw on a pair of sweatpants since he didn't
think he'd be going anywhere tonight. Between hot
water relaxing his muscles and the low hum of the
AC, he was feeling lazy, and all he wanted to do was
fill his stomach and—after his dog came home—
hang out on the couch and do some channel surfing.

When he picked up his cell phone from the bed
where he'd tossed it before showering, he saw that
he'd missed a text message. For a moment, he was
tempted to ignore it—just toss the phone down and
go downstairs. He wasn't in the mood for a sum-
mons across the street and he was starving. But then

the camera spotted his face and unlocked enough to show him the notification.

It was from Gwen.

Smart move, running inside. It's a mess over here.

Guilt hit him and he dropped into the armchair in the corner of his room, which was usually just storage for sweaters or hoodies that he'd worn over shirts once or twice, so they weren't really dirty but also weren't clean enough to go back in a dresser drawer.

What's going on?

Evie watched a few YouTube videos and thinks she's a master plumber now, and Lane's trying to explain how drains work and she's not taking that well. Mom's in a weird mood and Mallory's mad because she was late picking up the boys from summer camp and had to pay a fee because Lane's truck was blocking in all three cars because of the Sheetrock delivery and he had his keys in his pocket and wouldn't come upstairs until he was done with some science thing he was doing in the cellar.

Case pictured Gwen furiously typing all that into her phone with her thumbs and couldn't help smiling, though it faded quickly. She had a lot on her plate, obviously, and despite having a great sense of humor, she probably wouldn't find his amusement funny.

Is there some way I can help?

He really didn't want to get dressed again and go over there, but if she needed him, he would in a heartbeat.

No. Save yourself. Stay hidden and lock your doors.

He laughed. You people have my dog.

We do? There was just enough pause for the panic to set in—where the hell was Boomer?—before another message came through.

I'm kidding. He's with Jack and Eli in the house. They were trying to convince him to eat the summer reading assignments because they think "the dog ate my homework" actually works.

Boomer would eat a lot of things, including things he probably shouldn't sometimes, but Case didn't think Mallory's kids would have much luck getting him to eat their homework. Not without splattering the pages with some bacon grease, anyway.

I could have used Boomer today when I got attacked by a cat as thanks for trying to get her out of a tree.

Aren't you allergic to cats? That makes the scratches hurt even worse.

True story. He settled into the chair, content to put off dinner until the messages stopped coming. Sure, the phone was mobile, but he didn't want to divide his attention between preparing food and Gwen. All of his attention was on her.

Laura patched me up when I dropped off the truck.

I was going to offer to patch you up but Lane's mom stole my excuse for getting out of here.

Case groaned and fought down the urge to beat his head against the phone screen. He'd blown it. If he'd waited a minute before sending the second text message, Gwen would have been offering to tend his admittedly minor wounds in that moment. And he definitely would have taken her up on that offer.

I just got out of the shower, so I probably washed the ointment off. You could help me reapply it.

As soon as he sent it, he realized that invitation had sounded a lot sexier in his head.

Dammit. Lane told Evie to stick to taking pretty pictures and leave the decisions to him and she told him where to put his decisions and Mom is crying and everybody's yelling. Gotta go.

Good luck he sent back, and this time the little dots that told him she was responding didn't appear.

He'd come *this* close to being alone with Gwen, and in his own house, no less. Frustration made him drop his head against the hand-wash-only sweater that lived permanently on the back of the chair—a Christmas gift from Laura, who either didn't read the tag or had too much faith in Case's laundry capabilities—and closed his eyes.

It was tempting to jump back in the shower before the hot water heater recovered fully and see if the cold water helped any, but he'd tried that already and it did nothing to cool his desire for Gwen. He still thought about having sex with her. He just shivered while imagining it.

Then he heard Boomer bark, and he had to scramble downstairs and out to the front yard wearing nothing but gray sweatpants. Clearly the Sutton drama had spilled into the house, and if there was one thing his dog didn't like, it was angry voices. If offering his belly to be rubbed didn't help—or was ignored—he was out of there.

Either that or the dog's internal clock had told him it was time for his person to make dinner.

After looking both ways, he signaled for Boomer to cross the street. Crouching, he ruffled the dog's neck and asked him about his afternoon, getting a few enthusiastic face licks in return.

"I missed you, too, buddy. Let's go eat."

Boomer took off toward the house, and Case

chuckled as he followed. But as he reached his porch, he couldn't help looking back at the Sutton house. Gwen's window was empty, and he felt another pang of regret at how close he'd come to having her company tonight.

Maybe he'd get lucky and Evangeline would go up a tree again. Getting mauled by a cat and needing some TLC was a painful way to get Gwen across the street to his house, but at least they'd be alone.

Chapter Nine

It's Old Home Day, folks! As we gather to-gether to celebrate Stonefield on this gorgeous summer day, don't forget your sunscreen. The parade will depart from the school parking lot at ten o'clock sharp and make its way through town and around the square before returning to the school. The sidewalk sales and the events and vendors on the square will be ongoing until five o'clock, so pace yourselves! And don't for-get to fill out a "What I Love About Stonefield" card at the official Old Home Day booth! One very lucky resident will win a basket of gift cards from local businesses!

—Stonefield Gazette *Facebook Page*

"It's a beautiful day, isn't it?"

Her mother's cheeriness set Gwen's teeth on edge, but she forced a smile in response. "It is."

Sure, it *was* a beautiful day if one liked baking in the sun and wading through humidity that made the outdoors feel like a sauna. Gwen didn't, but she didn't have any choice but to stand behind the card table Case had borrowed from the thrift store and plaster a smile on her face. Mallory was overseeing Sutton's Seconds, since the sidewalk sales were a big part of their Old Home Day celebrations, and Ellen was flitting around. Lane had looked like he might vomit at the thought of standing at a booth all day, talking up the beer he was brewing to the public, so that left Gwen and Evie to take turns telling the good citizens of Stonefield how amazing Sutton's Place was going to be. Evie was definitely going to be better at that, but Gwen doing her part was only fair.

"People won't really start coming around until after the parade's over," Ellen continued, as if Gwen hadn't attended every Old Home Day celebration from birth until she finally escaped to Vermont.

"You should go watch the parade with Mallory, Mom," she suggested. "And she might need help setting up for the sidewalk sale."

"Oh, we finished that before I came over here."

Of course they had. When it came to the thrift shop, Ellen and Mallory were a great team because they'd been running it together for a long time. Unlike brewing beer and opening a tavern, Sutton's Seconds was totally in their wheelhouse.

"Do you need anything?" her mom asked. "There's water in the cooler under the table, and you put sunscreen on, right?"

"I'm wearing so much sunscreen I could play slip and slide without a hose and tarp right now." Ellen laughed, but she was looking around, and Gwen knew she was scoping out the booths and looking for her friends. "I've got this, Mom, if you want to go say hi to people."

"I'll come back and check on you. And remember, if anybody says anything about your books, you're just going to smile and nod."

Gwen pasted an obviously fake smile on her face and nodded, causing Ellen to sigh and throw her an exasperated look before walking away.

Left alone for what would probably only be a few minutes, Gwen straightened the stack of flyers Evie had printed up for the occasion. Because they didn't have an opening date yet, they'd kept it simple. The logo and an introductory paragraph. A few photos of the brewing in process—and Mallory had even managed to catch Lane smiling in one of them—and a list of where they could be followed on social media so they wouldn't miss any updates.

They'd also gotten an enthusiastic yes on the concept of having orders delivered from S-HoP, so there was a sign with both logos announcing the partnership, as well as a stack of take-out menus from the pizza place. Ellen had wondered about having a framed photo of David, but it was Mallory who found the words to gently explain to her that whichever of them was manning the booth would be accepting condolences and talking about their father all day instead of hyping their product.

Keeping her eyes on the flyers that didn't really need to be straightened again kept Gwen from scanning the slowly growing crowd, looking for Case. He'd be wandering somewhere, since D&T Tree Service didn't run a booth. Instead they carried on the tradition of their fathers of sponsoring a wood artist's booth. A guy who carved animals from wood with a chain saw. A couple who made the most gorgeous bowls out of chunks of wood with chisels. Always something that drew in spectators, who couldn't miss the large Sponsored by D&T Tree Service sign. That way they could be part of the celebration, but as Lane's dad had often said, it wasn't really something that needed a booth of its own. If you had a problem tree, you called a tree service.

The flyers didn't stop her from *thinking* about Case, though. She could needlessly fidget with paper and still relive their carriage house kisses. And she could remember all the Old Home Day celebrations of her youth, when she'd imagined what it would be like to be there with Case, walking hand in hand through the booths. In her youth, she'd dreamed of him buying her a flower from the garden club booth. Now she had a picture in her mind of her feeding him a bite of cotton candy and him sucking the spun sugar from her fingertips.

"Gwen!"

Jerking her head up as guiltily as if she'd been caught with her fingers actually in Case's mouth, Gwen saw Molly coming toward her and relaxed. "Hey, Molly."

"Your face is really flushed. I know it's hot, but it's not even noon yet. Maybe we could find some kind of umbrella? Or find a shady spot we can move the booth to."

Gwen laughed, relieved to have the heat in her cheeks blamed on the weather. "I'm just not used to being outside, I guess. But I'll be fine, and you know the shade spots are reserved for the beverage vendors and picnic tables."

"Okay, but if you need a break, just shoot me a text. It's not as if I have anything else to do today."

"What? There's no Cyrs Funeral Home booth? What fun is that?" They both laughed. "I guess being the only funeral home in town saves on the advertising budget."

Molly nodded. "We did get to be a part of it a few years ago, though. A parents' organization signed up to have a float and after they got approval, they asked Dad to drive the hearse in the parade with banners that said Free Ride If You Text And Drive."

"Mallory sent me pictures. Two of the car and four close-ups on the Old Home Day committee members as it drove by."

"Although we approve of the message," Molly said in a haughty, high-pitched tone, "we don't feel that your display was in keeping with the positive and uplifting community spirit the Stonefield Old Home Day celebration seeks to inspire. Of course, we will continue to welcome your participation as sponsors for future celebrations."

Gwen laughed. "Give us your money, but keep your deathmobile out of our parade."

"The next year, Mom wanted to sneak it into the parade so it was following the ambulance in line, but my dad talked her out of it."

"And that's why your mom is one of my favorite people in this town," Gwen said with a grin. "That and her pies, of course."

They talked for a few minutes before they heard Molly's name being called and she moved on to socialize with somebody else. Over the next hour, the parade segued from rescue vehicles to sports teams and Scouts mingled in with floats to the very long line of tractors they'd see again at the fair in the fall. By the time it got to the end, where the organizers put all the townspeople who were just really proud of their cars and trucks and wanted to show them off, a lot of people were already milling around in the square.

Gwen gave out flyers and talked about the beer—they'd had all the info and buzzwords drummed into their heads by Lane—and smiled and nodded. She'd been dreading the day, but it wasn't as bad as she'd feared. A few people mentioned *A Quaking of Aspens*, but mostly to tell her they'd enjoyed it or that they'd bought a signed copy from the library sale. She figured the people who were still mad about it would visit the booth later when Evie was behind the table.

As time passed and she started getting hungry, Gwen realized she had yet to see Evie, and she hoped her sister hadn't blown her off. Even if she snuck away to find food for a few minutes and let people take flyers on their own, there was no way she could stand the whole day manning the booth.

When she couldn't take it anymore, she took out her phone and pulled up Evie's contact page. Texts were easy to miss or ignore, and Gwen was starving, so she called her instead. Just when she thought she was going to end up going to voice mail, her sister answered.

"Gwen. Hi. I…" In the background, Gwen heard a male voice as Evie paused. "Sorry, I was doing something and lost track of time. I'll be right there."

She hung up without Gwen even saying a word, and as happy as she was that the freedom to find food was imminent, she found it odd. And it had been admittedly hard to tell, but she was fairly certain the voice she'd heard in the background was Lane's.

Sighing, she slid her phone back in her pocket. The exes had been working together reasonably well, for the most part, and she really hoped Evie hadn't been delayed because they'd gotten into an argument.

When Evie did appear, she looked flustered and wouldn't meet Gwen's eyes. "I'm sorry I left you holding down the fort for so long. I'll take over now."

"Must have been something good to make you lose track of time," Gwen said. She was fishing for a clue to what Evie had been up to, and she was careful to keep her tone light so it wouldn't come across as criticism.

Evie scoffed. "Good? I don't know about that. I ran into Lane and—"

She stopped talking abruptly and pressed her lips together, and Gwen arched an eyebrow. Did she not want to admit she'd been arguing with her ex? It wasn't as if they didn't all know a lot of turbulent water had flowed under that bridge.

"Whatever," Evie said, waving her hand in dismissal. Gwen wanted to push for more than a *whatever*, but then her sister's expression changed. "Uh-oh. Incoming, and I think it's ten degrees colder already."

Coming toward them was Daphne Fisk, Case's aunt on his mom's side. Unlike Laura—who was Case's aunt on his dad's side—Daphne was the kind of person who made the Wicked Witch of the West's theme song run through your head as she approached, and since Gwen had no place to hide, she could only hope Daphne was making her way toward an unseen person behind Gwen.

No such luck.

"Well, well… Gwen Sutton. It's been so long since

I've seen you, I almost didn't recognize you." Gwen recognized the not-so-subtle dig for what it was, but refrained from pointing out that Daphne had seen her at the funeral in January, when she offered Gwen the world's most awkward condolence hug.

·"It's nice to see you again, Daphne," Gwen said, and that was somewhat true. Once you got to know her and accepted that she could be a little abrasive at times, she was actually funny and could be kind when it was called for.

"When I saw on the *Gazette*'s Facebook page that you were back in town, I was surprised, but I'm sure it's wonderful for Ellen to have you all home again."

She refrained from pointing out she wasn't actually *home* because she lived in Vermont, but she didn't want to get into a battle of semantics with Daphne. Plus, since Stonefield was her hometown, she supposed the word would technically always apply, even if it made her itch.

"Will you stay in the house with Ellen, or are you looking for a place of your own?"

Taken aback by the question, it took Gwen a moment to remember that Daphne owned one of the two real estate offices in a neighboring town, and the question was probably a habit for somebody whose living depended on the buying and selling of homes. The positive aspects of her personality really shone when she was in selling mode.

"I'm not staying," she said. "I'm just here until

Sutton's Place is up and going—here, take a flyer—
and then I'm heading back to Vermont."

Daphne actually looked shocked, so maybe her
question hadn't been purely professional, after all.
"But look around you. All your friends and family
are here, and Stonefield House of Pizza was voted
Best Chicken Fingers in New Hampshire two years
in a row. Why on earth would you want to live anywhere else?"

Okay, the chicken fingers at S-HoP *were* the best
in the state, but Gwen wasn't sure she was the kind of
person who would put that at number two on the pro
list when considering where to live one's life. Plus
she didn't want the people of Stonefield thinking she
was moving back permanently, so she needed to nip
that rumor in the bud immediately.

And there was nobody better to spread that word
than Daphne Fisk. She was an incredibly big cog in
the rumor mill for somebody with iffy people skills.

The last thing Case expected to see as he wandered around the town square was Lane sitting on
a bench, bent over so his elbows were propped on
his knees and staring at his feet. Today should have
been a big day for Lane—a happy one, at least—but
his cousin looked as if he was sitting under a small
black rain cloud that was intent on ruining his day,
and only *his* day.

"Hey," he said as he reached the bench. Lane
looked up and judging by the scowl on his face and

the way his jaw was clenched, he definitely was not having a happy day. "I'd ask if your dog ran off and left you, but he's my dog. And he actually did run off and leave me, since he decided Jack and Eli were a better bet for dropped food, and I still don't look as down as you do."

"I ran into Evie and…well, you know how it is with Evie." Lane stood and took a deep breath, as if he was trying to force his body to relax.

Case wasn't sure exactly which aspect of *you know how it is with Evie* Lane was referring to. The two of them bickering was how it usually was, but there was also the way Lane was still in love with her—though he'd never admit that out loud. And the way Evie was always looking at Lane as though she had a lot she wanted to say to him, but wasn't sure how.

There were a *lot* of ways it could be with Evie when it came to Lane, but Case wasn't sure this was either the time or the place to dig any deeper on that one. "I'm surprised you're not at the booth. I've heard a lot of buzz about the brewery while I've been wandering, and it's all good. We should head over there."

Lane snorted. "Gwen called Evie to take her turn, so I think I'll wait awhile. In fact, I'm going to go check on some things back at the carriage house, and maybe by the time I'm done, it'll be Gwen's turn again."

So he was going to hide in his cellar again. Whatever it was that had happened, Case hoped they got over it quickly because full-on avoidance of each other wasn't going to work well for the Sutton's Place team. But he could see that the best thing for Lane right now was some alone time, so he nodded. "Let me know when you come back and I'll stop over."

Now abandoned by both his dog *and* his best friend, Case continued roaming the square alone. He stopped by the booth the tree service had sponsored this year and watched for a while. A woman who lived several towns away made birdhouses from scavenged, fallen wood and when he'd seen her videos on Facebook, he'd reached out about having a booth at the celebration. The crowd seemed to love watching her work—she told stories the entire time her hands moved—so there were a lot of eyeballs on their sponsorship sign and she'd probably sell some finished pieces. Another D&T Tree Service success. Marketing that didn't require any labor on his part was his favorite kind.

Moving on, he was aware he was getting closer to the Sutton's Place booth. There was a tingle of anticipation he couldn't ignore, even as he tried to remind himself Lane had said Evie would be taking a turn handing out the flyers.

Then, above all the noise, he heard Gwen's laugh and he swiveled toward the sound as if his body was on a string and her voice was tugging on the other end.

She was talking to Daphne, and Gwen's back was to him, so he couldn't see her face. Daphne wasn't really a people person and one of the kinder ways people tended to describe her was as *a little abrasive*, but she'd always liked the Sutton family. And Gwen had been laughing, which was a good sign.

He'd almost reached them when Gwen's voice rang out, clear as a bell and using what he thought of as her *emphatic* tone.

"I am absolutely not staying in this town a minute longer than I have to."

Case's step faltered and he stopped, giving himself a moment to absorb the definitiveness of her words. They shouldn't have been a surprise—he knew how she felt about Stonefield. But he was disappointed that spending time with her family—and two very hot kisses with the guy across the street—didn't appear to have softened her stance at all.

Not that he truly thought she would change her mind. He just wished she didn't have to sound quite so *sure* about it.

As he stood there, Evie scanned the crowd, and since she was facing Gwen, she could see him behind her. "Hey, Case."

Gwen spun just as he got his feet moving again, and he managed to get a smile on his face. "Hello, ladies."

"Hi," she said, and she started to take a step toward him before she stopped herself. "Having fun?"

Wondering if she'd subconsciously intended to give him a kiss hello before she remembered they were surrounded by people had distracted him too much to do anything more than nod at first, but then he realized all three women were watching him, so he cleared his throat. "It's a nice day for it, and the artisan at the tree service booth is amazing, so yeah, I'm having fun. Are you getting a lot of traffic?"

Gwen nodded. "Everybody can't wait to try the beer."

"Hey, it's my turn to watch the booth," Evie said. "You should go walk around with Case for a while and find some food."

She said the words casually enough, but he saw Gwen give her sister a *what are you doing?* look, which got a look of exaggerated innocence in response. Clearly he wasn't the only one who thought Gwen should spend some time with him this fine day.

"I could use a hot dog," he said in what he hoped was a casual, friendly way that didn't give away the *oh, please please please* he felt on the inside.

"And fries." She gave Evie and Daphne a quick wave and started walking away, leaving him to catch up. Either she was afraid something would come up and Evie would leave again, or she was *really* hungry.

They walked without talking for a few minutes, making their way toward the side of the square where the really good food truck was always parked. Throughout every year, the Old Home Day committee held fundraisers to pay for the food trucks, and one year when participation had been particularly low, they scrapped them. The only food available that year was the pulled pork sandwiches the volunteer fire department sold, cookies and brownies from the student council's bake sale, and judging the chili contest. The food truck fundraisers had been a rousing success ever since.

Case was wishing he had the courage to reach just a little to the right and take her hand in his when he realized she'd slowed down. Her gaze was locked onto a rack of cotton candy and, as he looked, she caught her bottom lip between her teeth, looking a million miles away.

"Do you want some cotton candy?" he asked, expecting her to laugh and tell him she'd outgrown spun sugar on a paper cone a long time ago, but her cheeks flushed. It was getting hotter by the hour and she'd been standing at that booth for a long time. "Or maybe some lemonade and we can sit in the shade for a while."

"I'm actually starving, so maybe some real food first." She smiled, and there was a naughty gleam in her eye he didn't understand, but was totally on board for. "Then the cotton candy."

Once they each had a fully loaded hot dog and a paper carton of fries with extra salt, they found an empty picnic table in the shade. He went back to get them each a cup of freshly squeezed lemonade and then sat across from her. Considering her hot dog was almost gone by the time he got back, she hadn't been lying when she said she was hungry.

"Have you seen Lane today?" she asked between bites.

"For a minute, earlier. He was heading back to the carriage house."

"Did he say anything about Evie?"

Since his cousin hadn't really told him anything, he supposed he wouldn't be breaking a confidence. "I'm guessing probably the same thing Evie said about Lane."

"Something happened. Maybe a fight."

Case wasn't so sure, but he didn't know one way or the other, so he nodded. "Probably."

"Hopefully it wasn't too bad, because getting this brewery up and running is hard enough without having to navigate them not being able to be in the same room." She held up a french fry, as if to make a point. "And speaking of being in the same room, Evie and I were talking last night, and we've been here for two weeks and haven't been in the cellar yet. We think we should get to see what all the fuss is about."

"That, you have to take up with Lane. For a laid-back guy, he's very controlling and a perfectionist when it comes to the brewing room. Nobody can touch it but him."

"Does he think we're going to start pushing buttons and dialing things and pulling levers?" He made a *well, maybe* face—mostly joking—and she laughed. "Well, Evie might. Especially after whatever happened between them today. But I think we have a right to see it."

"I agree. And since we're on the topic, you should stop by the popcorn vendor. I was over there earlier and noticed he upgraded to a bigger setup, so I asked him and he's looking to get rid of the machine he had last year. It would probably be a good size for the taproom."

"Why would we have a popcorn machine?"

Case shook his head, sighing. "It's like you've never even been in a bar, I swear. Having a popcorn machine is fun, plus it's salty. People who eat a lot of popcorn need another drink."

"I'll stop over there before I go give Evie a break," she said, digging into the fries again. "And I guess I should be the one who brings up the tour with Lane, rather than her."

He nodded, and they finished the fries together. He was about to ask her if she'd seen the birdhouses yet, and suggest they go see them before finding some cotton candy, when his phone buzzed in his pocket. He hoped it would be nothing, but when he pulled it out to read the message, he wanted to hurl the phone to the ground and jump up and down on it.

"Judging by your expression, it's not good news," Gwen said, and he shook his head.

"One of the selectmen thought it would be fun to use a drone to take overhead video of Old Home Day, and now his very expensive drone is stuck in a tree."

"They all just watched the big red fire truck with the very tall ladder go by in the parade, plus the selectmen see the town budget, so I'm pretty sure they know we have one of those in Stonefield."

He snorted as another text message followed the first. "Apparently the fire truck is too long to get into the space they have."

"Of course it is." Gwen smiled. "I guess I'll go talk to the popcorn guy and then head back to see how Evie's doing."

That's not at all what Case wanted to happen. He wanted to walk around the square with her more, even though he knew she wouldn't hold his hand out in public. Especially *this* public, since everybody would be talking about it before their fingers were even fully linked. But there was still nobody else here he wanted to spend the day with more than with her. There were booths to explore and games to play. He wanted to play them with her.

"Thanks for lunch," she said, standing and balling up her trash to toss in the can. "Maybe I'll run into you again."

"Definitely," he said, and the look that passed between them felt like a promise.

A promise doomed to be broken, as it turned out. The rest of the afternoon seemed to pass by in a blur of not talking to Gwen. By the time he'd gone to Laura's to get the boom truck and retrieved the drone, Gwen had gone to the thrift shop to give Mallory a break because Ellen was off with her friends. Then he hung out in a shady spot on the lawn with Jack, Eli and Boomer for a while because too much excitement and junk food had worn them all out. When they finally rallied and went off to have more fun—minus the junk food on strict orders from Case—Gwen was at the library, signing a few more books and talking to people.

Before he knew it, it was time to wrap up the celebration, and by the time he'd helped the birdhouse artisan break down and pack up her van, Gwen was gone. They never even got their cotton candy. To say he was disappointed was an understatement, and he and Boomer brought the big truck back to Laura's. When he'd swapped it for his pickup, though, with its excellent air-conditioning, the heat and activity of the day started catching up with him.

He meant to have a quick bite to eat and then text Gwen. Maybe they could sneak out to the carriage house for more stolen kisses. Or maybe, if he was *really* lucky, he could talk her into popping over to his house for a little while.

But as soon as he and Boomer hit the sofa, he was out. And by the time the dog's snoring and kicking feet from chasing something in his dreams woke Case from his accidental nap, the house across the street was quiet and Gwen's window was dark.

Maybe tomorrow, he told himself. Tomorrow he'd kiss her again.

Chapter Ten

*Good morning, Stonefield! Yesterday we cel-
ebrated a beautiful day on the town square, so
you know what that means. It's lost and found
time! The Old Home Day committee says it
was a record year for items left behind, so
if you're missing anything, stop by town hall
during business hours. Unless you lost several pocket-size bottles of bourbon. Those were
confiscated by the cleanup volunteers.*
　　　　　　　　—Stonefield Gazette *Facebook Page*

Case blinked at the text message from Lane that
had lit up his phone at an unreasonable hour on a
Sunday morning.

I have to give the women a tour of the cellar today.

Then he blinked at the clock and saw that it was almost eight thirty. So maybe not totally unreasonable, unless a person didn't fall back asleep until the wee hours because they were thinking about Gwen Sutton.

Thank you for updating me on your plans for the day.

He typed the response, hoping Lane would hear the sarcasm, and tossed the phone back onto the nightstand. It missed the wireless charging mat and bounced onto the floor.

It chimed a few seconds later, but he ignored it. Even though it was well past the time he usually got out of bed, he knew if he closed his eyes, he'd have no trouble going back to sleep. When the phone chimed again, he groaned.

Then he heard Boomer's footsteps padding up the hall and knew he'd be getting up in a few minutes. He had a dog door into the fenced backyard if he needed to get out, but Boomer much preferred the company of his person and once Case opened his eyes, he was fair game.

The dog jumped onto the bed and settled next to Case, staring down at him. And he had the cell phone in his mouth.

"Really, Boomer?" He took the phone, thankful the dog wasn't of the slobbering variety and read the text messages.

I want you to come with us.

Of course he did.

Please. The *please* was hard to ignore. Obviously Lane wasn't looking forward to hosting all four Sutton women in his brewing space. As he chuckled, another text message popped up in the thread.

Things are a little rough with Evie and me right now. I need all the buffers I can get.

What did you fight about yesterday?

The three dots hovered in the thread for a long time, appearing and disappearing, before another message came through.

Something stupid. We only fought because we almost kissed. Arguing was easier.

Case was wide-awake now. He'd known something had happened between them, but an almost-kiss had never crossed his mind.

Another text came through from Lane.

Mom's calling me. We're doing it at ten. Can you come?

It was just like his cousin to drop a bomb like that and then run. He'd say something and then regret saying it. The belated realization he didn't actually want to talk about it after all would bring an urgent excuse to leave the conversation.

I'll be there, Case sent back, even though he would rather have asked a million questions, starting and ending with "Dude, what were you thinking?" But either Laura needed him or Lane was lying about it to get out of explaining. Either way, he'd get no answers right now. He'd need to find a way to sneak a few minutes alone with his cousin later.

That was easier said than done. By the time he and Boomer got across the street, the women were already outside, giving Jack and Eli a list of chores to be done in the yard. The dog loved helping the boys with outdoor chores, so he knew where Boomer would be while they did the tour. There were definitely no dogs allowed in the cellar.

"Case is here," Ellen said loudly, waving her hands as if to herd them toward the carriage house door. "Laura and I are running to the city later for yarn, so let's go."

"Mom, really?" Mallory threw up her hands. "Where are you going to put more yarn? I think if you pulled all the skeins from all the places you've stashed them, you would actually have *more* than the yarn store."

They bickered about the necessity of just the right shade of blue she needed for a new project as they moved inside. They had to navigate around the stacks of Sheetrock that had been delivered but couldn't be hung yet because the electrician had gone to a cook-out the previous weekend and thought it would be a good idea to finish off the potato salad that had been sitting in the sun for three hours.

"I feel like we should have the code written down," Ellen said, as Lane reached for the digital keypad mounted on the frame of the glass door. "Just in case there's an emergency. Or you might forget something and it's easier to call and have one of us do it than drive all the way over here. But mostly in case there's an emergency."

"It's oh-eight-twelve," Lane said through gritted teeth.

Ellen smiled. "Well, that's easy enough to remember. It's Evie's birthday."

Case watched his cousin's jaw clench so hard, he was afraid it would lock in the position and tried to intercede. "Guess that was easy enough for David."

Ellen frowned. "But the keypad didn't go in until—"

She stopped talking abruptly, as if a light bulb illuminating in her mind had short-circuited her mouth, which made the moment even *more* awkward.

Lane had chosen Evie's birthday and now they all knew it. Plus, Ellen had squashed any chance they'd all assume David had chosen the date knowing, when he tried to unlock the door, he'd have a one-in-three chance of getting it right the first time. The silence stretched on until Gwen took charge of the moment, stepping forward and punching the code in. There was a slight click, and she pulled the glass door open before gesturing to Lane.

"After you, Mr. Head Brewer."

"Head Brewer, huh?" Lane said, arching an eyebrow.

"It sounds loftier than Mr. *Only* Brewer."

They all laughed, popping the tension like a bubble, as Lane went through the doorway. "Cool. Lofty was exactly what I was going for."

There was a lot of murmuring among the women as they descended into the cellar, and Case wasn't surprised. It looked totally different than the last time they'd been down those stairs, and this was the first time they were seeing the massive, intricate operation. The cellar was dominated now by huge steel tanks and hoses.

"Wow. I'm not sure what I expected, but it wasn't this," Gwen said.

"It's a seven-barrel system," Lane said, as if that would mean anything to them. "It's bigger than we really need right now, but David's goal was always distribution—at least statewide, if not New England—and it's a lot harder to expand an operation once it's up and running."

Once the tour started in earnest and Lane started throwing around words like *mash tun* and *sparging* and *fermenters*, Case tuned him out for the most part. Once Lane got going, he could be intense, and Case was more interested in drinking beer than knowing how it was made. And he'd like to keep it that way, because he was more than happy to help out with the start-up, but he had his own business to run.

He was also a lot more interested in watching Gwen than he was in listening to his cousin. Unlike him, she paid attention to every word Lane said, and he loved the look of concentration on her face. As much as he loved her smile and the sound of her laughter, the intense and studious look did it for him, too. It seemed there was nothing about her that didn't work for him.

And he really wanted to get her naked soon. *Very* soon.

Once the tour was over, they all went back upstairs except for Lane, who told them to make sure the door lock engaged on their way out. Case guessed it would be a while before his cousin emerged from the cellar. Until Evie was gone, at the earliest.

"I have a list of things I'd like to have done while I'm with Laura," Ellen said when they were milling around in the taproom again, and all three of her daughters sighed in unison. Case was impressed, but he guessed they had a lot of practice. "We've been so busy with the brewery that the house has been a bit neglected, so there's a chore list on the fridge. But I'll stop and pick up some ice cream on my way home."

"So we're children again," Gwen muttered as they began dispersing.

Case nudged her with his elbow. "But your mom's bringing you ice cream, so there are definitely benefits."

"I guess. She buys the so-called fun flavors that everybody loves, with chips and chunks and swirls, but she never buys plain chocolate ice cream. There's nothing wrong with a classic."

"Gwen, let's go," Evie called. "You're not getting out of this. You said doing mindless tasks helps you plot, so you're not getting out of it by claiming you have to work, either."

"I guess I should go," Gwen said, but at least she sounded reluctant. He hoped that was because she'd rather be with him than go dust the Sutton family knickknacks.

"I've got a chore list of my own," he said. "But maybe I'll see you later."

She smiled. "I hope so."

Case held on to those three simple words as he and Boomer did some yard work, and then he made a quick run to the store before moving inside to do some housecleaning. Boomer was a more enthusiastic helper for the outside tasks, and Case didn't blame him. Both of them preferred the outdoors, but laundry had to be done and the bathroom didn't scrub itself.

The dryer buzzed just as he finished his supper, so he went upstairs to put his laundry away, and when he looked out his window toward Gwen's—which was almost an involuntary response to walking into his bedroom at this point—he saw the whiteboard.

Rocky Road and Buttered Pecan. Yuck.

His run to the store earlier had been a spur-of-the-moment impulse, but Case loved it when a plan came together. He grabbed the Sharpie and the white poster board he'd felt silly buying earlier in the week and wrote a response.

I have plain chocolate in my freezer. The good stuff.

Her response made him laugh. *Don't make me come over there and take it.*

He could picture her face as clearly as if she was standing in his bedroom. That bossy expression that lost some of its oomph because she was also trying so hard not to smile at him. There was nothing he wanted more in that moment than to do exactly that—to make her come over there—and he grinned as he wrote the three words that were almost guaranteed to bring Gwen to his door.

I dare you.

He *dared* her?

So Case didn't think she had the nerve to walk across the street and show up at his door? Since they'd known each other for their entire lives, he really should know her better than that by now. Or maybe he did know that, and this dare was really an invitation. Gwen knew when she knocked on his door that there was a good chance she was going to end up in his bed.

She was so tired of fighting it. She was tired of constantly reminding herself why it was a bad idea to get any more involved with Case than she already was. And more than anything, she was tired of lying awake at night with her body aching for his touch.

So she was going to walk across the street and feel his touch. And then she was going to eat his ice cream. Or maybe she'd have the dessert first, and then him. The order didn't really matter, but she was staying until she'd had both.

The words were easy enough to say to herself when she was staring at her reflection in her bathroom mirror, but by the time she'd snuck out of the house—carefully avoiding every squeaky board by muscle memory—to dodge answering any questions and was on his front porch, she had a serious case of nerves. She could only hope she wasn't trembling enough to make her hair bounce.

She knocked, and then smiled when she heard a single *woof* in response before Boomer's nose pressed up against the living room window. Maybe it was her imagination, but she'd swear the dog smiled back at her.

Then the door opened, and Case was standing in front of her, looking sexy as hell and a little bit smug. He moved aside to let her in, and then closed the door. She stepped back to lean against it, folding her arms across her chest.

"I can't believe you dared me to come steal your ice cream," she said in a low, husky voice that made heat flare in his eyes.

"You never could resist a dare." He reached past her and she heard the dead bolt click. "And now we're alone. Behind a locked door. And did I mention we're alone?"

She liked that they weren't even going to pretend the ice cream was anything but a ploy to get her into his house. There would be no wasting time dancing around the subject and wondering who would make the first move, and when and how.

Her hands went to his waist without any conscious thought on her part, and he braced his hands on the door—one on either side of her head, so he was looking down at her. The hunger she felt was reflected in his eyes and she shivered in anticipation.

"Maybe I should make you show me the ice cream first," she said, sliding her hands up his back, because she didn't intend to actually let him walk to the freezer.

"Proof of chocolate?" His eyebrow arched. "You don't trust me?"

"I don't trust anybody when it comes to chocolate ice cream."

She was just about to bring an end to the banter by rising up on her toes to kiss him when she felt a thump against her hip and looked down to see Boomer gazing up at her, waiting to be greeted. Chuckling, she reached a hand down, rubbing his ears and giving his head a scratch.

"Hi, Boomer," she said.

She was afraid the moment was lost and now they'd break apart. The ice cream would come out, and as much as she wanted that, she wanted Case more. He never moved, though, and when Boomer had his fill of hello pets and wandered away, Case's arms were still braced on either side of her.

Rather than risk another interruption, Gwen lifted her hand to the back of his neck and drew his mouth to hers. It felt as if every moment between the last time their lips touched and now—all the yearning and imagining and wanting—went into the kiss, and she wrapped her arms around his neck, just wanting to hold him even closer.

She made a squeaking sound against his lips when he reached down and hooked his hands behind her thighs, lifting her against the door. Wrapping her legs around his waist, she held on to his neck even tighter. But as his tongue danced over hers, she relaxed against the door and loosened her grip enough to run her fingers through his hair.

But when he shifted, trying to pull her T-shirt up enough to work his hand under it, she started to slide, and he yelped when her fingers tightened and yanked the hair she'd been caressing.

Tightening his hold on her, he leaned in again so her back was once again pressed firmly against the door. She was lower now, though, which made their positions awkward, and the fact they were both laughing didn't help any.

She was never going to forgive him if she had to explain an emergency room trip to her family. There wasn't enough chocolate ice cream in the world.

"I've always wondered how the whole *up against*

the wall thing works," Case said, and his shoulders shook as he struggled to stop laughing. "And I think it probably works better if the clothes come off *first.*"

"Maybe we should take this upstairs before one of us gets hurt."

After making sure he had a good grip on her, Case took a step back and waited until her feet were solidly on the floor before letting her go.

He didn't totally let her go. As if afraid she might change her mind, he laced his fingers through her and led her up the stairs and to the bedroom on the front of the house, facing hers. She noticed the poster board leaned up against his dresser, as well as the Sharpie on top, and smiled.

She was still smiling when he pulled his shirt over his head and tossed it aside. When he arched an eyebrow at her, she did the same, dropped her shirt on the floor. Heat flared in his eyes as he took in the lacy white bra she'd put on after her shower. It wasn't particularly fancy, but he made her feel like she was wearing the finest lingerie money could buy.

When he picked her up and set her on the end of the mattress, she laughed again and scooted up to the pillows before pulling him on top of her. His mouth claimed hers, and she ran her hands up his back, loving the feel of his muscles rippling under her touch. He kissed her harder and then moved to plant a kiss at the corner of her mouth. Her jaw. Just under her jaw.

Gwen turned her head, exposing her neck to him,

but when she opened her eyes, she saw Boomer sitting just inside the bedroom door. He was watching them, and when Case's teeth nipped at her skin, she jumped a little. Boomer's head tilted, one ear sticking up, and he gave her a look that made it clear he wanted to know what she and his person were up to.

Gwen pushed against Case, stopping his exploration of her collarbone. "I totally get that this is *his* house and I'm just a guest, but your dog is staring at me and it's a little weird."

"Yeah, that's a *lot* weird. Boomer, go sleep on the couch." After making an annoyed huffing sound, the dog ambled out of the bedroom. "Problem solved."

"I was ignoring him until he did the head tilt thing and looked confused." She rolled her eyes when Case tilted his head, just like Boomer had. "I'm not sure how I feel about you having company in here so often, your dog's trained to give you privacy."

Case laughed. "Sometimes that dog has gas so bad, one of us has to leave the room, and his name's not on the tax bill, so it ain't gonna be me. Now, where were we?"

Gwen was ready to hit fast-forward. "We were getting rid of the rest of these clothes."

"I think you're cheating," he said. "But I want you naked, so I'm going to let you get away with it."

It felt like only seconds before their clothes were on the floor and the full, naked length of his body pressed down on her. She savored the weight of him, her fingernails skimming his flesh as he cupped her breast and teased the taut nipple with his tongue. And when he closed his mouth over it and sucked, his tongue swirling, she gasped. Her back arched and she felt the hard length of his erection pressing against her.

She wanted him. "Now, Case."

Being Case, he ignored her and took his time teasing her. Her breasts. A light, tickling kiss on her stomach. His hands roaming her body as he worked his way lower, until his teeth nipped at the inside of her thigh. Then his mouth was on her, and she fisted her hands in his hair as he slid his tongue over her sensitive flesh and sucked gently at her clit.

But Gwen wanted to feel him inside of her *now*. Everything else could wait until she wasn't on fire with need. "Case, I want you now."

He lifted his head and, after kissing her thigh and then her stomach, grinned at her. "You always want to be the boss, Gwen."

"I need you. I've been waiting…forever." She didn't even want to tell him how long she'd been imagining this moment.

He snagged a condom from the bedside table and, once it was on, he settled over her. But he wasn't done tasting her yet, and he licked and sucked her nipples until she was squirming.

Finally he reached between them and guided himself into her. Slowly, his body trembling with restraint, he moved his hips, rocking a little farther into her with each thrust. She pushed against him until he filled her.

Case was still for a moment, his forehead resting against hers, but she didn't want him in control. She wanted him to *lose* control, giving them both what they wanted. Scraping her nails down his back, she pressed her hand to the curve of his ass and urged him to move, lifting her hips.

With a groan, he pulled back and then thrust into her, so deeply she gasped. Stroke after stroke, he moved within her, and she ran her hands over his body. His skin was hot under her hands, and she lifted her head, kissing him as his thrusts quickened. Faster. Harder. Deeper.

She let her head fall back against the pillow and whispered his name as the orgasm came, but in her head she screamed it as wave after wave of pleasure took her.

He groaned and the muscles in his back tightened under her hands as he came, his body pulsing jerkily, until he collapsed on top of her.

His breath was hot and fast against her ear, and she turned her head enough to kiss his rough cheek. He made an appreciative sound and kissed her neck. They slowly caught their breath and after a couple of minutes he rolled away. With her eyes still closed, she felt him get out of bed, but he was back before she'd summoned the energy to open them again.

Until he pulled her close and kissed her on the mouth. Then she opened her eyes and smiled up at him. He was propped on his elbow, and he kissed her again before he let his head drop to the pillow next to hers.

"You're not going to put this in a book, are you?"

The question surprised a chuckle out of her. "I snuck my notebook under the pillow. You didn't see me taking notes?"

"That must have been when I had my eyes closed, trying to picture box scores and algebra equations to, uh…slow things down, if you know what I mean."

"How can I *not* use that in a book?" She wouldn't, but if he was going to dish out the teasing, he was going to take it, as well.

"It's gotta be worth a whole chapter, at least." He kissed the side of her neck, his mouth lingering there so he could probably feel the way her pulse quickened. "Maybe two."

Chapter Eleven

Happy Monday, everybody! This morning the Old Home Day committee asked the town clerk to draw a "What I love about Stonefield" card from the box and the winner of a basket of gift cards from local businesses is Paul Jenkins! Usually we share what the winner loves about our town, but his favorite spot in town is very personal to him and his wife. Congratulations, Paul! And our friends at the Stonefield Police Department offer a friendly reminder that public indecency is against the law.

—Stonefield Gazette *Facebook Post*

Case opened his eyes to find Boomer standing next to the bed, staring down at him, with his front paws on the mattress. For a few seconds, he was confused because the dog wasn't shy about jumping on the bed, but then his brain was jolted fully awake by memories of last night flooding through his mind.

Making love to Gwen. Her sitting on his couch in nothing but one of his T-shirts while they ate chocolate ice cream straight from the carton. Making love to her again.

Boomer was standing next to the bed staring at him because Gwen was in the dog's spot. Thank goodness Boomer was a creature of habit, though, because Case had forgotten to turn his alarm on before he fell asleep. He kept an alarm clock next to his bed instead of using the alarm on his phone because he absolutely hated forgetting to shut it off and getting woken up at five thirty on a holiday Monday.

Sliding out of bed as quietly as he could, he pulled on a pair of sweatpants and gestured for Boomer to follow him out of the room. Even though he had to go to work, there was no reason to wake Gwen. It wasn't as if she couldn't find her way home from here.

After brewing a first cup of coffee, he heard footsteps upstairs, so he hit the brew button on a second cup. He'd just finished fixing them and setting them on the table when Gwen came down the stairs. Her T-shirt was inside out and she was rocking some serious bedhead, but what really caught his attention was the utter panic on her face.

"I didn't mean to go to sleep. How am I supposed to sneak back in now?"

He sat and took a sip of his coffee, gesturing at the one he'd made for her. "Well, you're an adult, so you could try just walking through the front door because you're free to do whatever you want."

As she sat, she shot him a look that let him know in no uncertain terms that she wasn't about to do that, and his high spirits sank a little. Would it really be that bad if her family knew she'd spent the night at his house? "I don't want to answer a million questions about us. Or even one question."

"Is this still about me dating Mallory in high school?"

She snorted and waved her hand. "No, you were right about that. It's just easier if nobody knows."

Easier for her maybe. "So tell them you got up early and wanted to ask me something about the brewery."

"They would never believe I was up and dressed and out of the house before my mother even got out of bed." She took a sip of coffee and then sighed. "They're used to me sleeping later than they do, so I'll just wait until Mom and Mallory and the boys leave, because I can probably sneak by Evie. She'll either be in her room or be staring at her phone."

After downing half his coffee, he pushed back from the table and stood. "I have to get ready for work, but feel free to sit here and hide."

She must have heard the bite in his tone because he only made it halfway across the kitchen before she spoke. "Case, wait. I'm sorry. I realize how it sounds, but it's not about you and me. I'm not sorry I got to wake up beside you. But there's so much going on and there's no…break from it. And I don't want this added to the conversational chaos I've been living in over there."

The earnestness in her eyes softened him. "I get it. I mean, I'm not thrilled about being some secret you have to keep from our friends and family, but I also know how they can be."

"And how this town is."

He realized that was part of it, too. While they joked about last night ending up in one of her books, it was something she'd experienced in Stonefield—people seeing themselves in the pages of her books and not being happy about it. Gossip about Gwen Sutton would spread like wildfire, and the locals probably wouldn't be shy about asking her if Case was going to be in her next book. It would be embarrassing and incredibly awkward for her.

But he didn't think that was all of it. If she was really into him as much as he wished she was, Gwen might still want to keep them a secret from the town as much as possible, but she wouldn't be so stressed about hiding it from her family. She might be clinging to the upheaval in her family's lives the way she'd tried to use his past relationship with Mallory—as a reason to keep him at a distance because she wasn't staying, and everybody knowing about them would just make it messier when she left. For now, though, he was content to let it be.

"I do have to get dressed, though," he said. "Just drink your coffee and relax, and I'll be down in a few minutes."

Since he generally took his showers in the evening, thanks to his job, it didn't take him long to throw on some clothes and brush his teeth. As he was heading back down the stairs, he heard the slamming of car doors across the street and knew Ellen and Mallory were leaving to drop the boys at their summer day camp before opening the thrift shop. In a few minutes it would be safe for Gwen to sneak across the street as though she'd done something wrong.

Boomer came in through the dog door at the same time Case entered the kitchen. The dog knew that Case getting dressed meant it was almost time to get in the truck, so if he had any pressing business to take care of in the yard, he'd best get to it.

Gwen was still sitting at the table, half of her coffee gone. She had a faraway look on her face, but at least she didn't look panicked anymore. Last night had been amazing, and he wanted to part ways this morning on a more positive note.

Actually, what he really wanted to do was call in sick and crawl back into bed, taking Gwen with him. But he was the boss and he couldn't afford to have the guys slacking off because he wasn't there. Not with Lane already doing light hours.

But seeing her in his kitchen with his dog, who was enjoying having a lady in the house to scratch his ears, tempted him so much, he almost pulled his phone out of his pocket. One phone call and a little white lie to Laura and he could take her back to bed and make love to her again.

Right up until she realized Evie, at least, would wonder where she was and panicked again. Then, rather than spend the day alone being mad about it, he'd show up late to work in a foul mood. Leaving on a higher note now was still the better choice, he decided.

"I hate to leave, but I have to get to work. I'd play hooky, but with Lane gone so much, we're already busting ass to stay caught up." After downing the rest of his coffee, he grabbed his keys and his wallet. "Take your time drinking your coffee, though. You can make another one if you want, and feel free to rummage in the fridge. Just lock the door when you go."

"Thank you. I'm sorry I was a mess when I woke up." She gave him a sheepish smile. "I hope if you think about me while you're at work today, you think about last night instead of this morning."

"Oh, I'm definitely going to think about you." He leaned down and gave her a very thorough kiss good morning.

"But not when you're up in a tree," she said. He smiled and gave her another thorough kiss—this one a kiss goodbye. "Or when you're running the chipper."

"I promise I'll think about you safely. Let's go to

work, Boomer." The dog was obviously reluctant to leave her, but after a mournful sigh, he went to the door. Before he opened it, he turned back to Gwen. "Just so you know before you try to be sneaky, your T-shirt's on inside-out."

Of course she hadn't made it past Evie, because that's just how Gwen's luck went. Her youngest sister happened to be walking through the living room— and her eyes were *not* glued to her phone—when Gwen crept onto the porch and squeezed through the front door without opening it wide enough to trigger the squeak in the hinges.

"Good morning," Evie had said, in a questioning tone made even worse by the amusement and curiosity dancing in her eyes.

"I went for a walk," Gwen said. "Walking helps get the ideas flowing when I'm stuck."

"I hope you don't need too many ideas, then, because it's not that long of a walk from Case's house to ours." When Gwen tried to muster a fake look of indignation, Evie laughed. "You're wearing the same clothes you were last night, and because I love you, I'm not going to mention your hair."

"You can't tell anybody," she said, running her hand over her hair. Yeah, it was bad.

"That's not fun at all. And how am I supposed to keep this a secret from Mallory?"

"It's pretty simple. You just don't tell her. You know they both assumed I was still in bed when they left, so there's no reason for the subject to come up at all."

"It's not like everybody didn't see it coming. It won't be a shock."

Gwen glared at Evie, who was enjoying this way too much for so early in the morning. "I don't think *everybody* saw it coming. I mean, Mal, maybe. I told her we'd kissed a couple of times, but…sometimes people kiss, Evie."

"Sure." Evie nodded. "People just randomly kiss all the time."

She was clearly not awake enough yet to win this battle with her sister, so she went upstairs—ignoring the sound of Evie's laughter following her to the second floor—where she took a shower and put on clean clothes. After checking her email and finding nothing urgent, she went back downstairs for a second cup of coffee and another shot at swearing her sister to silence.

"Evie, I—" she started as she walked into the kitchen, but she broke off when her sister held up her hand.

"I'm not going to tell anybody," Evie said. "I was just messing with you because it's fun to wind you up. But I won't lie if Mom or Mal asks me outright, though I can't see any reason why they would."

"Thank you," she said as she fixed herself a cup of coffee. "It's not that I feel a need to hide it. I just don't want everybody talking about it."

"If it makes you feel better, I'll share a secret

with you," Evie said quietly, slowly swirling her half-empty juice glass.

Gwen pulled out a chair and sat. "Mutually assured destruction by gossip?"

Evie smiled. "Something like that."

"Let's hear it, then."

"I almost kissed Lane."

And Gwen almost dropped her coffee mug. As it was, she froze with it halfway to her mouth and then had to carefully set it back on the table. "What? When?"

"At Old Home Day."

Gwen leaned back in her chair, trying to make sense of it. "I knew something had happened, of course, but we—Case and I—assumed you'd gotten in a fight."

"We got in a fight to hide the fact we wanted to kiss each other."

Gwen took a long sip of her coffee, giving herself a moment to think so she didn't say anything careless. As amused as Evie had been earlier, she looked anything but that now. And for good reason. She'd almost kissed her ex-husband, who was now her mother's business partner.

"You guys always had that kind of chemistry," Gwen said. "It makes sense that you still do, but now you know that chemistry isn't enough and that you two don't work on any other level."

"I know." Evie shook her head and then her face cleared as if she'd literally driven thoughts of kissing

Lane out of her mind with the motion. "The electrician called Mom this morning and said he's feeling better and would be here today. And before we stopped speaking to each other, Lane said the bar top is ready and he's going to get it this afternoon."

"Today's my day to research prices and figure out if it makes more sense for us to drive to the city and buy food for the menu at one of the stores there or have it shipped." Not a super fun task for somebody who'd gotten as little sleep as she had. "I think it's going to tip in favor of us doing the shopping because we don't have enough refrigeration space to order in bulk."

"Them."

Gwen frowned. "What?"

"You said it would tip in favor of *us* doing the shopping, but it will be Mom and Mallory because we won't be here."

"Of course." She knew that. It wasn't as if she'd forgotten she wanted Stonefield in her rearview mirror, but until she left, they were a team. But she could see the urge to get out of town in her sister's eyes and knew Evie was itching to put a lot of miles between her and whatever was going on with Lane. "Whatever we set up has to be sustainable for Mom and Mal—and Lane, I might add, because he can do more than brew the beer—without us. Or Case, though he's always going to be willing to help."

He was just that kind of guy. He had a good heart, and Gwen cringed when she thought of how he'd tried to hide his reaction to her words this morning. He said he understood, but she knew her urgent need to hide their relationship from her family had hurt him.

Maybe it was for the best. There was a possibility that they'd gotten each other out of their systems last night, and now a little distance would bring their fling to a natural and relatively painless end. It wasn't a *probability*, but it was possible. She wasn't sure when it was going to happen, but her leaving Stonefield was inevitable. If some awkwardness between them now saved harder feelings later, she should let it be.

But when she went upstairs to get her laptop and the list of ingredients she was going to research, she couldn't help looking out her window, into the bedroom where she'd spent the night. Maybe losing sleep because she'd been in his bed was good for the muse, she admitted to herself, because the idea she'd gotten Case out of her system was the best piece of fiction she'd come up with in a long time.

Chapter Twelve

Mrs. Monroe has asked us to let our readers know that, as much as she appreciates everybody's concern for her cat Lemon, to please stop assuming Lemon is a stray and "rescuing" her. Lemon is adventurous and likes to visit people around the neighborhood, and Mrs. Monroe has had to retrieve her from the shelter numerous times this month. We're sharing a photo of Lemon, so if you see her, please assume she's just out being social.

—Stonefield Gazette *Facebook Page*

Gwen closed her laptop with a satisfied sigh that seemed to come from deep in her soul. The wheels had finally started turning in her head, which got the words flowing. Not only was it a relief on a professional level, but it was good to have a creative outlet to distract her from the fact it had been two and a half weeks since she'd woken up in Case's bed and she'd barely seen him since.

Between the tree service, working on the renovations, and Lane chasing permits and inspections, the guys were exhausted. Other than a Fourth of July cookout, they were so busy and so tired, they weren't even taking Ellen up on her open invitation to join them for meals.

Gwen missed Case, even though she'd had plenty to keep her busy. While the men worked with the contractors to help keep the costs down, the women researched suppliers and argued about glassware. They went over the regulations for the food and safety certificates until Gwen was sure she could recite them from memory. And when she could, she wrote.

For the past three days she'd done the bare minimum the brewery needed in favor of writing, and she was so close to finishing the book now, she wanted to lock her door and not leave her room until it was done.

But a girl needed to eat. She also needed to stretch out the kinks in her muscles because the old rocking chair might be beloved, but it wasn't exactly ergonomic.

She was almost to the stairs when she heard a sniffling sound from the master bedroom and saw that the light was on. Her mom should have been at the thrift store, so the concern something was wrong drew Gwen to the door.

But it wasn't Ellen. As she stepped into the room, Gwen saw Evie standing still with tears running down her cheeks as she stared at the fist-sized whelk shell her sister had found on a vacation to Cape Cod when they were kids. Rather than going on a shelf in Evie's room, it had sat on their father's dresser all these years.

"I remember that trip," Gwen said quietly. "It was the summer before you started first grade. We found so many shells that they were everywhere in the car and right after we got back, a heat wave started and the car started to smell so bad, Mom refused to drive it until every shell was found."

That made Evie smile. "Dad paid us a dime each for every shell we found. I cried because you got more dimes than me, so Mal gave me some of hers."

That sounded like Mallory. "But that shell rode home in the glove box, wrapped in paper towels so it wouldn't break."

"He told me it had to stay in here and only he could pick it up because it's so fragile and he knew I'd be sad if it broke, but really it was because he made the ocean sounds, so if he wasn't with me, I wouldn't hear the ocean."

"When did you figure out it was him?"

Evie smiled. "I always knew it was him, from the very first time. It made him happy, so I pretended to believe him."

"He was surprisingly good at it."

"He really was." And then, as Gwen watched, Evie's face crumpled and more tears spilled over onto her sister's cheeks as she put the shell to her ear and spoke in a broken whisper. "It's just silent now."

She hated when Evie cried. Her little sister had been born a sunny bundle of happiness and so rarely got upset that her tears felt extra wrenching to Gwen somehow. Moving to Evie's right side, she bent slightly so her face was closer to the shell and started making ocean sounds. She was going for waves crashing on the shore, but it sounded a little more like she was fishing for stations on an old AM radio.

Evie made a sound that was like a hiccup and a sob combined, and then she started giggling. Gwen did her best to maintain the bad ocean sound, but it wasn't long before they were both giggling. And she was relieved to see that, when Evie wiped tears away, they were tears of laughter and not sorrow.

"I guess being able to mimic waves isn't one of those hereditary skills, like curling your tongue," Gwen said when she could breathe again. Evie immediately stuck out her tongue, curling up the sides until her tongue made a perfect tube, and then she grinned triumphantly. "Show off. I swear, I didn't inherit any of the fun stuff."

"You inherited Dad's habit of making up stories," her sister said. "And then, unlike Dad, you made a career out of it. Nobody pays me to roll my tongue."

"There's probably somebody on the internet who would pay to watch you do that," Gwen pointed out, and Evie laughed again before gently putting the shell back in its spot on Dad's dresser.

Gwen held her breath as her sister ran a finger over the curve of the shell, but when Evie turned back to her, she was smiling. The tears had passed. And as their gazes met, her sister shook her head. "You really are the worst at ocean sounds. But I love you, anyway."

"I love you, too, even though you have a weird tongue." And then Evie stepped forward and Gwen wrapped her arms around her. It felt good to hug her sister, and they stood together in their parents' bedroom until she felt the tension ease from not only Evie's body but her own.

"You're still in your pajamas," Evie pointed out as she released her.

"One of the perks of my job." She followed her sister out of the room and down the stairs to the kitchen. "I'm just getting a quick snack and taking it back to my room before I forget what I was going to write next."

"Food in your bedroom?" Evie gave an exaggerated gasp and clutched her chest.

"Don't tell Mom," Gwen called as she grabbed a bag of chips and a bottle of water and fled the kitchen.

"I'm going to need a spreadsheet to keep track of the secrets I'm keeping for you," Evie shouted after her.

Once back in her room, Gwen set the bag on the table and settled herself back in the rocker with her laptop without letting herself go to her window. It would be pointless anyway, since Case was at work, but mostly she was doing her best not to let thoughts of him creep into her head, where they could drown out how she was going to wrap up a plot thread still dangling in her manuscript.

Still, she itched to call him. Or send him a text message. They'd barely had any time to talk since she'd done her walk of shame across the street, and she missed him. And that was why she didn't let herself pick up her phone. Realizing she missed him when it was simply being busy that kept them from having time alone made her realize she was *really* going to miss him when she went home to Vermont.

That scared her. Her longtime crush and succumbing to the chemistry sizzling between them was one thing. Those feelings weren't supposed to become anything more, but missing him was a feeling. And thinking about how hard it would be to leave him was *definitely* a feeling.

Because it was easier to worry about dangling plot threads than obsess about whether sleeping with Case had been a huge mistake, Gwen opened her laptop and started typing.

"I can't believe how much you guys have gotten done."

Ellen's voice echoed through the taproom, surprising Case and almost causing him to smash his thumb with the hammer he'd been swinging for two hours. He'd known the electrician since middle school and they'd managed to knock a little off the estimate by offering up Case to do menial tasks—like nailing in the staples that neatened and secured all the wiring run through the walls. He could definitely use a break, he thought as he set the hammer down and moved his arm to stretch the muscles.

Much to his disappointment, Ellen hadn't brought Gwen with her, but she had brought lemonade, which he accepted with gratitude. "We're getting there."

"Is Lane still downstairs?" she asked, setting the other lemonade on the edge of the bar, which was still covered in paper and plastic to protect it.

"Funny how that beer has to be babysat when there's manual labor to be done," he teased, and then he immediately regretted it when her expression changed. "That was just a joke, Ellen. I give him a hard time, but I'm just teasing."

Her relief was evident, but there was still some tension around her eyes and mouth. "I know we've asked a lot of you, Case. But I'd rather lose the house and the thrift shop than have this come between you two boys."

"The thrift shop?"

"David took out loans against both properties," she said. "I thought you knew that."

He hadn't. He wasn't sure Lane did, either. No wonder she looked exhausted. She really could lose everything.

Since she looked like a woman who could use a hug, he set his lemonade down and wrapped his arms around her shoulders. "I promise it won't come between us. Lane and I are okay, and that's not going to change. And you're keeping your thrift shop and absolutely not losing this house. Boomer and I don't want new neighbors."

After giving him a tight squeeze and releasing him, Ellen smiled and looked around the open space. Case hadn't been lying. They *were* getting somewhere, and it was starting to look like a real taproom.

"When do the lights go up?"

He took a long gulp of lemonade before joining her in the middle of the room. "Not yet, but all those boxes mark where the lights, switches and outlets and whatnot will go. After the Sheetrock is hung, they cut it out around the boxes, but the lights won't be hung until after that process is done."

"There are a *lot* of boxes."

Case chuckled, because she was definitely right about that. "The plan calls for being able to have different light configurations. The industrial-look dropdowns you chose will hang over where the tables are going to sit—and look amazing, I might add—but there wil! be recessed cans around the outer walls. Those probably won't be on often, but you'll be able to move the tables under those lights if you host an event that requires space in the middle of the floor for dancing or bridal shower games or…whatever."

"Hosting events," Ellen murmured, doing a slow turn. "I bet it was David who thought of that and not Lane."

"I wouldn't bet against you. But Evie's running with it. She's got pages of ideas going, and she spends a lot of time looking at the social media of other places, seeing what works for them. Speaking of, keep your eye out for any great Halloween costumes that might come into the thrift shop."

She laughed, and then they roamed around while he showed her some of the construction items that had been crossed off the to-do list. It wasn't easy to concentrate, though, because a part of Case's attention was focused on the door, waiting for Gwen to come through and see what her mother was up to. Two and a half weeks with only quick glances, short brewery-related conversations and no physical contact was almost as hard on him as the schedule he'd been keeping.

She didn't show up, though, and eventually Case couldn't keep it in anymore. "I'm surprised Gwen's not out here with you. What's she up to?"

He thought he'd asked it casually enough, but the amused look that crossed Ellen's face could only be described as *knowing*. "She's been in her room, writing. Evie said she left her room a couple of times for snacks during the day, and then we saw her briefly for dinner. She was still in her pajamas and I don't think she actually brushed her hair before putting it up, plus she has that faraway look that means she's not actually listening to anybody. She must be getting near the end."

Case nodded, smiling to hide the disappointment. He was happy for Gwen. He knew she'd been stressed about the book and he was glad she was writing, but he wanted to see her. Ideally he'd like to see her somewhere they could both be naked, but at this point, he'd settle for just getting to spend time with her.

In the weeks since they'd made love, she seemed to be trying to put their relationship back in the no-sex box in which they were longtime friends who shared sizzling glances when nobody else was looking. Case didn't like that box, and he had no intention of letting them be shoved back into it.

Or maybe she was just busy with her book and the brewery, and he was reading too much into it. The last thing he wanted to do was get in the way of her writing, so he'd wait a little longer.

"Did you boys already eat?" Ellen asked. "I didn't realize you were out here or I would have called you in to eat with us."

"We ate before we came over." It was ravioli from a can, which he wasn't going to admit to her, but technically they'd eaten.

"Where's Boomer?" she asked. "He's not down-stairs, is he?"

Case laughed. "No dogs allowed down there. Not even Boomer. He made a friend at the job we were on today and that puppy ran him ragged. He barely lifted his head when I told him I was going out, and he was drooling on the couch when I left."

"It's good for him." Ellen looked around the tap-room one last time and then smiled. "I'll get out of your way. Promise me you won't work too late. You already worked a full day and now you're hammering away over here."

"Probably just another hour or so. We're not over-doing it."

After giving him a pointed glance meant to tell him they'd better not be, she left, and Case finished his lemonade before picking up his hammer again. He'd only pounded in a few wire staples when Lane emerged from the cellar, looking pleased with himself.

"Everything's going well, and right on schedule, too."

Case nodded, because when Lane said everything was going well and was right on schedule, he meant the brewing. While he understood his cousin's focus on the beer, since a brewery without beer wasn't going to make a lot of money, he also needed him to focus on the taproom, because without that, he and Lane were just going to end up drinking a *lot* of beer.

"Ellen just left. I gave her an update, and she brought lemonade."

Lane drained half the cup before setting it back on the bar. Then he rummaged in the tool bucket for another hammer. After pushing his hair back from his face—Lane really needed to make time for a hair-cut—he gave a weary sigh. "I think if we hustle, we can have this wire all nailed up tonight."

They worked in silence, focused on the task at hand, until the last loop of wire was secured. It didn't take as long as Case had feared, but he still needed to wrap it up and get back to Boomer. He'd been lis-tening for the bark that signaled the dog wanted to join him across the street, but there had been a lot of hammering, and he hoped Boomer was as tuckered out as he'd looked earlier.

As they finished cleaning up, Case looked at Lane, who looked even more exhausted than he felt. "If I tell you we don't need you on the job tomorrow at all, will you spend that time catching up on some sleep, or will you just use the time off to stress and work extra over here?"

Lane snorted. "Until this place is open and there are people in here paying to drink those brews, I don't think not stressing is an option. I'm okay, and I'll be ready to work in the morning."

"You can't keep going like this, Lane. I don't want to mother hen you, but I'm starting to worry."

"I told you I'm fine."

"And I don't believe you," Case said. "Don't make me sic Ellen on you."

"Okay, so I'm tired. And there's a lot riding on this, so it's on my mind constantly." Lane looked around the taproom. "But I feel good about it. I don't know if it makes any sense, but it's worth it. I think this part is hard, but that it's going to be awesome."

"I think it will be, too." Case wasn't lying. As it started to take shape, he felt in his gut that Sutton's Place was going to be a success. The beer was not only good, but the place would have Lane's passion and David's heart, and he could see it becoming a gathering place for Stonefield. "Just know your limits."

Lane nodded. "I met a guy in college who was into brewing beer. He didn't really have any place to do it himself, but he was learning everything he could about it, same as I was. For *someday*, we both said."

"Probably not easy to hide that kind of setup in a dorm room."

Lane chuckled. "I met him while *I* was there, but he wasn't a student. He was a cowboy, actually—worked on some huge ranch and he was in town for something. Some of the guys and I went out to a bar and I ran into him. Started talking. I saw him a few more times while I was out there, and we've kept in touch some since then, off and on. And I was telling David about him and that's how I found out he was really into brewing, too. We were always talking about it, and then we started experimenting on a small scale. He was always writing notes in that journal of his, for someday."

"You've done more than your share of talking about it over the years, too," Case pointed out. "You might not have taken copious notes but you've been planning this in your head for years."

"I should give Irish—the cowboy—a call and tell him I'm actually doing it, and that if he's ever out this way, he should stop by and check it out."

Case nodded, but he wasn't sure how likely that was. Lane had gone to the University of Montana to earn a BS in forestry because it was cheaper than staying in New England for his degree, so no matter where his old brew buddy was going, New Hampshire was going to be out of his way.

"The point is," Lane continued, "whether it was

Irish or David, we spent a lot of time talking about *someday*, and that someday is here for me now. Under the exhaustion and the stress, I'm about as happy as I've ever been."

"Then I'm happy for you." Just as Case slapped his hand against Lane's shoulder, he heard Boomer bark. "That's my cue to wrap it up."

"I'll close up here. Thanks again for the help."

When he got outside, Boomer was sitting patiently on the sidewalk, waiting for him. Rather than stand and wait for a signal to cross, though, the dog turned back when he spotted Case. He wasn't looking to visit the Suttons. He just wanted his person home.

Before they went inside, Case couldn't help looking back at the Sutton house, though. Light was shining from Gwen's window, so he took for granted she was still writing. As much as he wanted to hear her voice, or at least exchange a few text messages, he didn't want to break her train of thought if she was on a roll, so he sighed and went inside.

He'd be patient—for now. But he wasn't letting her shove them back in that damn box.

Chapter Thirteen

*We have a message from the Stonefield Police
Department to whoever keeps stealing the High
Street sign: Another one is being installed this
week (the fifth this year alone) and they are
installing a camera to keep an eye on it. No,
you won't be able to find the camera. But if
you steal the sign, they'll be able to find you.*
　　　　　　　—Stonefield Gazette *Facebook Page*

Gwen tried to tell herself she was imagining the
tension in the taproom this morning. She'd been up
until almost two in the morning writing, and she'd
discovered the hard way that her two rambunctious
nephews didn't magically sleep in or discover their
inside voices just because their aunt had missed her

bedtime. And there was no summer camp on Saturdays, so the yelling wasn't temporary.

Over the years, Laura had filled in at the thrift shop once in a while if Ellen was sick or just needed a Saturday off. Today was one of those days, because her mom hadn't slept well and was out of sorts.

Gwen knew the feeling.

Despite not having enough sleep, she had joined her mother and sisters. They'd scrounged several boxes of glasses from the thrift shop that could stand in for the real glasses they'd ordered. Evie had suggested, since there wasn't a lot they could do until the Sheetrock was done, that they use the glasses to make sure the bartender could work efficiently and that everything would work in reality the way it had on paper. If they needed anything changed—shelves moved or things rearranged—it was their last chance to do it.

It had sounded like a fun activity at first, but the mood was off today and after paying close attention for a few minutes, Gwen realized it was Ellen. Her mom was more tense than usual, and her eyes looked slightly puffy—as if she'd cried not long ago or hadn't slept at all.

Ellen took a glass out of the box, and Gwen waited for it to be handed off to be put on the shelf behind the bar, but her mom only stared at it, turning it in her hands. When the silence stretched on, she realized her mom wasn't checking out the glass and didn't appear to even be seeing it.

"Mom?" she asked, worry making her throat feel

tight. Ellen looked up at her, her expression blank. "Are you okay?"

She slowly shook her head. "No, not really."

"We can handle this, Mom. Why don't you go inside and relax for a while?"

"That won't help."

"Do you not feel good?" Evie asked. "You said you were feeling out of sorts, but are you sick or…?"

Her sister let the question die away as Ellen shook her head again, more emphatically. At a loss, Gwen started to reach out for the glass because her mother's hands were shaking, but she stopped when Ellen started talking.

"The night before our wedding, my mother told me to put five dollars away every week and to never touch it unless it was literally the only money that could put food in my kids' mouths. I did that. Every single week, even if I had to scrounge for change in the car and the couch cushions, I put that five dollars away. Eventually I opened a savings account for it because you can only keep so much money in coffee cans." She paused, taking a long, slow breath. "Once you girls were older, I stopped thinking of it as emergency money and more as a retirement vacation fund."

Gwen was already mentally reviewing what around them could be used as tissues because they were all about to be awash in Ellen's grief that they'd never get to take that vacation together. But tears didn't come. Her mother's face reddened and her chest heaved from deep breathing that looked a lot like trying to contain rage.

"I gave him that money toward the up-front costs," Ellen continued. "Over ten thousand dollars. He told me he'd give it back with interest within two years and that two years in would be a perfect time to leave the business in Lane's hands and take me away for a month to wherever I wanted to go. And it's all gone. *He's* gone."

"Mom," Mallory said quietly, but then nothing else because she didn't seem to know what to say. None of them did.

"This was his dream. *But I had dreams, too.*"

Gwen glanced at her sisters, only to find they were looking at her as though being the oldest gave her some kind of insight into what the hell she was supposed to do here. She had no idea.

"I'm so angry," Ellen shouted, and they all gasped when she threw the glass against the unfinished wall and it shattered against a stud. "And then I feel guilty about being angry because he died and he's not here anymore. But you know what? I'm still mad at him."

After taking another of the cheap glasses out of the thrift store box, Gwen passed it to Evie, who slipped it into her mother's hand.

"I'm so angry everything we worked for our whole lives is on the line and I don't feel financially secure." The glass flew through the air and landed in a glittering pile of shards over the first. Evie put another glass in her hand. "I'm so angry my daughters had to put their own lives on hold because their father put us in this position."

Another glass. "I'm so angry that at a time of my life when I should be starting to relax, I'm going to have to essentially work *two* jobs."

Through the corner of her eye, Gwen saw a shadow fill the doorway—she wasn't sure if it was Case or Lane—and she gave a quick shake of her head. The shadow receded as she handed Evie another glass, which she put in Ellen's hand.

Smash. "I'm angry that the one time I ignored my mother's advice and touched that money, everything went to hell."

Evie gave her another glass. This time her mom didn't throw it right away, but her hand was so tight around the base, Gwen was afraid she was going to squeeze too hard and slice her hand open when it broke.

But then Ellen drew her arm back and let it fly. "And I'm most angry that even if this place is successful beyond his wildest dreams and I get that ten thousand dollars back, my vacation plans are ruined because David's not here. No matter what I do now, the dream *I* had can never come true because he died and it's *not fair.*"

Evie held another glass at the ready, but Ellen didn't take it. Gwen braced herself for the tears that would surely come now, but when her mom's shoulders started shaking, it was from trying to contain laughter. She couldn't stop it, and suddenly the four of them were in a hollowed-out carriage house, surrounded by shattered glass, laughing together.

"Good lord, that felt good," Ellen said after a few minutes, wiping tears from her eyes. "But what a mess."

"You know sweeping is a mindless chore that helps my mind spin stories," Gwen said, looking around the floor. "I might be able to finish this book *and* start the next one."

More laughter, and then Ellen sighed. "I shouldn't have put all that on you girls, though. I've been trying to be strong, but..."

"Mom." Evie stepped forward, putting her arms around Ellen. "You don't have to be strong for us. We're here to be strong for *you*—to be strong for each other. We're your safe space."

"Always," Gwen said as she and Mallory wrapped their arms around their mom and Evie.

The group hug helped, she thought, soaking it in. There had been so much talk about them being in this thing together, but the embrace was a bond that surpassed words. She could *feel* their strength coming together as a family and it was deeply comforting.

"Okay, you girls go find something to keep you busy while I clean this mess up," Ellen said, pulling back. They all started objecting, but she held up a hand to cut them off. "That was a lot. I've been holding that in a long time, I think I need some quiet alone time to finish processing it."

Gwen understood that completely and, after finding an empty box for the glass, she and her sisters went outside. They stood for a moment, uncertain of what to do.

"If there's nothing else, I think I'm going to take the boys to the pool," Mallory said quietly. "They'll have friends there and I could do a few laps."

"I'm going to go work on the social media plan for a while," Evie said.

Gwen nodded before they walked away, though she didn't announce her plan because she didn't really have one. She knew herself enough to know if she opened her laptop right now, she'd just stare at the blinking cursor.

What she needed was a hug. As a rule, she wasn't a hugger, but having her arms around her family had felt so good. She'd gotten comfort from it, but mostly she'd been offering it. Right now she wanted arms wrapped around *her*. She wanted Case's arms—his strong body holding her.

And then she heard her name.

Case waited for her in the gazebo.

When he'd crossed the street and gotten close enough to the carriage house to hear yelling and glass smashing, his first thought was that the sisters—probably Gwen and Evie—were having some kind of terrible fight. But then he'd realized it was Ellen's voice, and he'd slowed his pace rather than rushing into the building to break it up.

The sight of Ellen smashing a glass against the

wall while letting her emotions out had told him what he needed to know, and even before Gwen had shaken her head to let him know it was under control, he'd started backing away. Ellen clearly needed to work through some things, and she had her daughters with her. He had no place in that moment.

But when they came outside and Mallory and Evie walked away, leaving Gwen standing there alone, he couldn't take it anymore. There seemed to be some assumption on everybody's part that because she wasn't as expressive with her emotions and always seemed to be in control, that she wasn't just as messy on the inside as they were at any given time.

He knew better, though, so he called her name and savored the way she almost managed a smile when she saw him. He was sitting on the bench built in all the way around the gazebo wall rather than at the picnic table, and he turned sideways as she entered.

Boomer picked his head up from his napping spot, probably hoping somebody had brought a picnic lunch, but when he saw Gwen's hands were empty, he flopped back down.

Gwen walked right to Case and he settled her on his lap, wrapping his arms tightly around her and resting his cheek on the top of her head. They didn't talk and it wasn't the most comfortable position for him, but he didn't care. He could feel some of the tension seeping out of her body as he held her, so he'd hold her for as long as it took to help her feel better.

"That was a lot," she said finally, but she didn't try to get up.

"It sounded like a lot. Looked like it, too."

"I'm glad, though. I think Mom really needed that." She chuckled and lifted her head. "I'm also glad it happened before we got the *real* glasses in."

Perhaps realizing a gazebo bench wasn't the most comfortable spot there was, Gwen pushed herself up and, when he swung his feet to the floor, she sat beside him. Case would have preferred to keep holding her—an aching back and legs were a small price to pay to have Gwen in his arms—but he reached over and laced his fingers through hers instead.

He'd been telling himself for days that the next time he had Gwen alone, they were going to talk. He didn't like being in this limbo of not knowing if they were starting something together or not, and he definitely didn't like hoping they were if she had her mind set on pretending nothing had happened.

But it didn't take an emotional genius to see that now wasn't the right time. All four of the Sutton women needed a break right now, and that he could do.

"Want to go for a ride?" he asked, guessing that Ellen wanted some time alone, and that Gwen wouldn't want to go inside with the rest of her family.

"Sure."

He chuckled, squeezing her hand. "You're not even going to ask where we're going?"

"No, as long as it's somewhere I can be in jeans and sneakers."

"I'm pretty sure there's nowhere in Stonefield you can't go in jeans and sneakers."

She grinned and bumped him with her shoulder. "That's true."

Once they were in his truck, with Boomer content to sit in the back seat—though he kept poking his head over the center console in case he was missing something—Case decided to keep it simple. The last thing he wanted was for them to walk around town and have her run into anybody with strong opinions about the book or movie, so he drove down a network of back roads to one of Boomer's favorite spots.

The river that ran around the outskirts of town was shallow and slow-moving here, running through a wide clearing in the woods. It was a fun and safe place for Boomer to run around, and he could play in the water to his heart's content.

"This is a beautiful spot," Gwen said, watching the dog splash through the river. "How come I've never been here before?"

"It's actually private property, so it doesn't get a lot of traffic, but I do tree work for the owner and he loves Boomer, so we have an open invitation." He looked at her and grinned. "Plus, you were probably afraid all those books you were always toting around might get wet."

She laughed and the sound filled the clearing. "That's a good point. I've never really been the outdoorsy type."

They were quiet for a few minutes, watching

Boomer live his best life. Every once in a while, she'd turn her face up to the sun and close her eyes, and he could practically see the stress seeping out of her muscles.

Then she looked at him and he could see that she still had a lot on her mind. And judging by the way her face softened as she sighed, it had to do with him.

"I haven't been avoiding you," she said quietly. "I know it probably looks that way, but I've been working."

He smiled, because it was good to hear her say it. "I hear you've been spotted wandering the house looking for snacks in your pajamas with messy hair, so I assume the writing's going well?"

She laughed, shaking her head. "Yes, it is. If there are crumbs on my pajamas and possibly also in my hair, the writing is going *very* well."

"Your job looks a lot more glamorous on TV. Lunches in the city and champagne toasts when the book is done."

"I usually celebrate finishing a book by taking a shower, sleeping for two days and then wondering when I stopped buying vegetables."

He was about to make a joke about her needing somebody to take care of her, but he realized at the last second it might sound like he was fishing for it to be *him*. And maybe he was, but he'd already decided today wasn't the day for that. She was finally relaxed and enjoying herself, and the last thing he wanted was for her expression to tighten up again because he'd brought up their relationship.

And maybe, before he brought it up, he should get hold of his own feelings on the matter. Yes, he wanted her. He wanted to spend time with her. He wanted her in his bed again. He wanted to hug her when she needed one, and he wanted to make her laugh.

But he'd just made a big leap from wanting to see her to being there to make her take a shower and eat vegetables while she was writing a book.

To be there for that, they'd be sharing a life together. Living together. He'd gone from zero to a hundred without any rational thought on the matter, and maybe before he brought Gwen into it, he needed to slow himself down.

No matter how *right* this felt in the moment, there were two pesky facts he couldn't just wave away because he liked being with her.

Gwen hated being in Stonefield and couldn't wait to leave.

He loved his life in Stonefield and couldn't see himself living anywhere else.

"I'm glad you're finding the time—and peace—to write," he said. "And there's definitely a lot going on, so I'm not going to pressure you. I mean, I'm going to keep chocolate ice cream in my freezer on the off chance I can lure you across the street again, but you don't need to worry about me. We're just enjoying each other's company. No pressure."

Case knew he'd said the right thing when her face lit up and she gave him a smile that heated his blood before she bent to take the stick that Boomer brought her.

"He likes when you throw it in the river," he told her, his voice sounding so rough he cleared his throat. "Sometimes he brings back a different stick than the one you threw, but we think it's rude to point it out."

"Good to know." She threw the stick and it hadn't even hit the water before Boomer was bounding into the river after it.

He lost track of how many times Gwen threw sticks into the river, but she was laughing and clearly enjoying herself, so he didn't care. After a while, he sat on one of the flatter boulders at the river's edge to watch them.

As much as some of the weight had been lifted off of Gwen's shoulders—at least temporarily—he could feel it pressing down on him. This is what he wanted his life to look like, and he ached to join in their fun. To pull her into his arms and kiss her. To tell her he hadn't been totally honest with her—that he wanted to be more than just friends enjoying each other's company.

Maybe even to ask if she was softening toward Stonefield now that she'd been back for a while.

But that wasn't why he'd brought her here. She needed room to breathe and he wouldn't encroach on that space. Instead he watched the woman he was falling in love with throw sticks to his dog and kept his mouth shut.

Chapter Fourteen

We hear there's been a lot of activity at the Sutton house this past week! There's a lot of buzz about the new establishment in town, and we'll announce their opening date as soon as we have it. Hopefully pictures, too, if they invite us over for a beer. In the meantime, we'll be bringing you updates about Sutton's Place Brewery & Tavern as we get them!
— Stonefield Gazette *Facebook Page*

"I hate painting," Gwen muttered to herself as she tried to pour paint into a rolling pan without getting it everywhere.

"So you've said," Evie muttered back. "At least a dozen times since breakfast."

Apparently, neither of them were very good at muttering to themselves. "Calling it a painting party doesn't make it any more fun."

"On that we agree. If you're going to call it a party, it should involve gifts, cake, cocktails or bacon-wrapped hors d'oeuvres."

"Or all of the above."

"I did bring doughnuts, though," Molly pointed out. "And some of them had sprinkles."

"We can always count on you to make it a party, Molly," Evie said, and they laughed.

Gwen took her rolling pan to her assigned wall and then grabbed one of the long rollers with the extension handles her mother had assembled. They were all there—they'd even barred Lane from escaping to the cellar—so hopefully it wouldn't take long, but the loss of yet another day still irked her.

It had been over a week since the incident with the glasses and her trip to the river with Case and Boomer, and during the entire time, she'd managed to write maybe ten pages and she was probably going to have to scrap eight of them.

It had been going so well and then…nothing. The writing wheels in her head had ground to a near halt and she couldn't figure out how to fix it.

Maybe, subconsciously, she'd been thrown off by her mother's emotional outburst more than she'd thought. Or maybe it was because it was the last weekend in July and she didn't feel any closer to going home to Vermont, despite her early resolve to be back by August at the latest. This—the carriage house and navigating her family's emotions and trying not to let her feelings for Case get too messy—was beginning to feel like her new reality, and it wasn't a reality of her own choosing.

Three days ago, she'd finally caved and talked to her agent—by phone, not email, which made it so much harder—and she'd been given another short extension. But he and the editor had made it clear that they were doing as much as they could because of her family situation, but if she didn't hand in her manuscript by the new deadline, they would have to delay the book's release, which would mess up production and flush the sales and marketing plan down the toilet.

She'd gotten off the phone relieved to have a reprieve and determined now that she'd straightened that out, to make the book a much higher priority in her life. Her family didn't even have an opening date for the brewery yet, thanks to waiting on inspections and permits and whatever else Lane needed for his binder of paperwork. They could spare her for a few hours per day.

Then Mallory had called to ask her to throw the roast and veggies into the slow cooker because she'd forgotten. And then Evie called because she'd driven into the city to buy a new printer and some other supplies, so they wouldn't have to outsource those things, but she'd misjudged all the box sizes and it didn't all fit in her Jeep. She was standing in the parking lot with it all until Gwen drove the forty minutes to put some of it in her car.

And so it went, day after day, until she wanted to scream. She'd even been tempted to lock herself in the cellar and hide behind a big tank with her phone off, but she knew Lane would find her eventually and she'd have to listen to a lecture on the sanctity of the brewing process.

"Um, Gwen, honey." She heard her mother's voice and stopped rolling.

"What do you need?"

"I need for you to stop attacking that wall and flinging paint everywhere."

Gwen frowned and really looked at the wall she'd been painting. Rather than the neat rows on Mallory's wall, which were already drying and blending into a creamy covering, Gwen's wall was covered in thick, uneven strokes that went in all different directions and were already drying into jagged streaks. And she was definitely making a mess of the plastic-covered floor around her.

"Sorry. I can fix it."

"You're always so particular about things. I thought you'd be better at this," Ellen said, her voice heavy with an amusement Gwen didn't share.

"Maybe this is why I'm a writer and not a painter," she said, hating the sullen tone, but unable to stop herself. "Or I used to be a writer, anyway."

"Gwen, if you need to take a break, you should. There are plenty of us to do the painting."

"No, I'm sorry." Everybody was working so hard

that, as much as she resented losing time to work, she couldn't put extra on their plates. "I get cranky when I'm not writing."

The guilt on her mother's face made Gwen feel like a jerk. "I know we've asked a lot."

"It's not just that," she said quickly. "You know I struggle here in Stonefield. Do you know when I went into the pharmacy the other day because I was out of vitamins, the teenager who was stocking the shelves asked me if I was the one who'd made Mrs. Dorsey look bad in the movie."

"You should be flattered, honey. They love talking about your books—especially *A Quaking of Aspens*."

Gwen snorted, which earned her a stern maternal look. "Flattered? They've accused me of fictionally murdering Tony Bickford and they think I accused S-HoP of food poisoning their customers. And I wasn't even the one who wrote that scene."

"Everybody was so excited for you when you got published, and then when everybody started talking about it and the book was on TV, it became one of the biggest things to happen for Stonefield, and I think everybody just wanted to feel like they were a part of it. I guess with a book, you do that by looking for yourself in it. And then the movie happened."

"Of course growing up in this town influenced me when I was creating a *fictional* town for my book. How could it not? But it *is* fiction." Gwen shook her head. "And even if somebody in the book was very heavily inspired by somebody here, I can't tell them that."

"I understand that," Ellen said, though Gwen

wasn't sure she truly did. "You can't change them, but you can choose how you let it affect you. Instead of being annoyed by the comments, maybe just appreciate their somewhat clumsy attempts at being a part of the excitement."

That almost made sense to Gwen, but being annoyed by the people in her hometown was a hard habit to break. "It doesn't matter, anyway. As soon as the brewery is open, I'm leaving."

"But—"

"Mom!" Gwen stopped, taking a breath because that had been louder than she'd intended and she absolutely was not going to raise her voice to her mother. "I have to go home, Mom. I haven't written at all for days. Other than a few stretches that went well, it's been almost impossible for me to work consistently. There's always something to do or somebody talking to me about something. And even if I lock myself in my room, there's so much going on that it's impossible for me to focus."

"It won't always be like this. Things will calm down."

There was no point in arguing because she wasn't going to be able to make her mother understand. There was always something. Somebody in the family always needed something. Friends always wanted to go do things. People felt free to talk to her about her books—especially what they didn't like about them. In Vermont, she had a routine. It was a lonely routine at times, but it was quiet. Peaceful. She'd written two books there in less time than it took her to write *A Quaking of Aspens* because she'd made herself a life in an environment that supported her career.

Stonefield was not that environment. The Sutton house was *definitely* not that environment.

And then there was Case. He was a distraction whether he was standing in front of her or not. She thought about him constantly—wondering what he was doing and when she'd get to see him again—and remembering the night they'd spent together kept her awake at night.

After a heavy sigh, Gwen refilled her paint tray and set about fixing the wall. It took her longer to make it look right than if she'd just calmed down and done it right the first time, but she was finally able to set her roller down and stretch her back.

"You have paint in your hair," Case said as he appeared at her side with two bottles of water.

She laughed and pushed some strands back from her face before taking one of the bottles. "So do you."

"I think I got in the way of the spray when you were taking all of your frustrations out on the paint roller earlier."

"Not my finest moment," she admitted before taking a long drink of the cold water. Then she looked around the taproom, which looked entirely different with the walls painted. It was brighter and warmer, and she could almost picture what it would look like when it was finished. "It looks so different."

"This is going to be a really nice place," he said,

and then he smiled at her and his eyes crinkled and her hands ached to touch him.

Sometimes keeping busy and being tired could keep her longing for Case under control, but there were times—like now—when the desire was almost a pain that she'd do anything to ease.

"Don't keep looking at me like that if you don't mean it," he warned in a low, rough voice before he reached out and brushed loose strands of her hair away from her face. His thumb grazed her cheek, the touch lingering, until everything faded away except for the feel of his skin against hers.

"Aunt Gwen!"

And her nephews' voices, yelling her name in unison. She sighed, dropping her head as Case laughed and took a step back. This family was going to be the death of her.

"Gram is going to start the grill, so she wants me and Eli to help you clean up," her nephew said, before turning to Case. "She said it's out of propane, though, and wants to know if you have a spare tank instead of Lane going to have it filled."

"I have one," Case said, and Eli took off to let Ellen know, while Jack very carefully started pouring the leftover paint from Gwen's tray back into the open gallon can. Then Case winked at Gwen and left her to finish the job at hand.

"You're the messiest painter, Auntie," Jack said, scowling as he picked up the roller handle with two fingers.

She laughed and bent to take it from him. "You're right about that. But let's get it cleaned up so we can have burgers."

"You look happy," Molly said as she sat on the gazebo bench next to Case.

He nodded. "We got a lot done today and now I have a cheeseburger. Life is good."

"Bacon cheeseburgers, even."

"It was until I gave Boomer my bacon. He's got a sad face that's hard to resist."

"I'd offer to share the bacon from mine with you, but I have no problem resisting your sad face." She smiled when he tried it. And failed, even though he batted his eyelashes a couple of times. "I don't think you could do a true sad face right now, anyway. You're definitely happy. Not just a cheeseburger happy, but a really loving-your-life-right-now kind of happy."

"Like I said, life is good," he said, taking a bite of his bacon-less burger.

"How much of that is because of Gwen?" she asked, and he almost choked.

Thankfully, he didn't actually inhale the bite, and chewing and swallowing it gave him time to think about the conversational curveball Molly had just thrown at him. It was a ball he wouldn't be able to field no matter how long he chewed, though, because he didn't know how to answer it. "It's nice to have all the Sutton sisters home."

When she laughed, he knew she wasn't buying what he was trying to sell her. "Nice try, Case. But this is me you're talking to. I know what's going on."

"Then you know more than I do," he muttered. Sometimes he barely got to see Gwen, and when he did, she was so distant he assumed the night she'd spent in his bed had been a onetime thing, after all. But then she'd go and look at him the way she had in the taproom a little while ago and he was all tied up in knots again.

"I like you two together," she said. "I mean, I haven't really gotten to *see* you together, but I've known you both my entire life and I think it's great."

"You do, huh?" He wasn't sure what Molly was basing that on, exactly, but it was nice to have somebody cheering for them to be a couple. It would be better if it was Gwen, but he'd take what encouragement he could get.

Looking across the yard, he watched Gwen talking with her nephews. They were showing her the derby cars they were making for a pinewood derby at day camp—something they worked on all summer when it was raining or the heat index was too high to run around outside—and her face was animated as she examined them.

"Oh, there's Mal. I need to ask her about something. I'll be back."

He smiled as Molly went off to talk to Mallory because he wasn't even sure if she needed to ask her about anything at all. Molly never sat still for very long. And she probably got the itch to move faster when she was sitting next to somebody who was ignoring her in favor of pining for a woman who kept stealing glances back at him.

Maybe Gwen was pining for him, too.

He watched her until Gwen glanced his way again, and he grinned and nodded his head slightly toward the empty seat next to him. She smiled back and then said something to the boys before heading his way.

When she sat down on the bench, it was close enough so their arms brushed and her leg rested against his. "Did you see the cars the boys are making?"

He nodded. "They're doing a good job. Lane and I usually try to be there for derby day, since we're a sponsor—the center buys the car kits so the parents don't have to—and it's always a fun day."

"When do they do that?"

"Usually late August, when they're wrapping up camp because school will be starting soon." When she only nodded, he realized she'd thought about going to watch and now they were both very aware she probably wouldn't be around for the derby day if she had her way.

"They send me pictures," she said quietly. "But that's the first time I've ever had them show me the cars."

"They're not really supposed to bring them home because then they forget to bring them back," he said. "I heard Jack say he was going to ask if he could break the rules just this once, though, because he wanted you to see them."

She chuckled. "I don't want them to get disqualified."

"It's not really *that* competitive," he promised.

When she reached up to push her hair back again, her finger caught in a clump of paint and she winced. "I wish Mom had let us clean up before starting dinner."

"She probably knew if we all scattered and took showers and then sat for a minute in the air-conditioning, she'd play hell getting us all gathered together outside again."

"True. It was hot today." She turned and gave him that little smile that brought a heat no air conditioner could cool. "Do you still have chocolate ice cream in your freezer?"

"I told you I would."

"I wasn't sure if you'd eaten it by now. By yourself."

"It's not as satisfying eating ice cream alone. I might have snuck a few quick bites here and there, but mostly I'm saving it for you."

She laughed, her cheeks flushing a soft pink. "Are we still talking about ice cream?"

"I'm not sure, to be honest." He laughed. "It works on so many levels."

After taking a deep breath, she locked her gaze with his. "Feel like company later?"

"Yes." He didn't even have to think about it.

"I'll stop over for some ice cream later, then, once

everything's cleaned up and everybody's settled into whatever they're doing tonight."

"If you're thinking about using some shrubbery to disguise yourself as a bush and sneak your way to my porch, be careful crossing the street."

She laughed and slapped his thigh and then let her hand linger there. "I was actually thinking I might just walk across the street because I'm a grown woman and I can do what I want."

Even as distracted as he was by the very welcome sensation of her hand on his leg, Case recognized her words as a big step for her. She was going to cross the street to visit him without trying to hide it from her family.

"I'll probably wash the paint out of my hair first," she continued, and he laughed with her.

He didn't care if she had paint in her hair or not. All that mattered to him was Gwen was willing to *not* hide the fact they had a relationship outside of working together on Sutton's Place. She wasn't hiring a skywriter, of course, but it wouldn't be long before word got around and she knew it. It was a big step for her.

And he'd make sure tonight was definitely worth it.

Chapter Fifteen

The Hall family would like to thank Dave Wagner for finding their beloved ferret, who slipped from his harness during his daily walk. And Dave would like to thank the Stonefield Police Department for responding so quickly when he called them because he was (and we quote) "just screaming like that goat on the internet because something furry ran over my face while I was watching the ball game." The ferret is safely back in the Halls' home and Dave's eye has almost stopped twitching.
—Stonefield Gazette *Facebook Page*

Having spotted Boomer's nose pressed against the window, Gwen wasn't surprised when the door opened before she even had a chance to knock. Case's welcome smile shifted into an amused grin, complete with raised eyebrow, when he saw her.

"Can I borrow your shower?" she asked, holding up her tote bag.

"Absolutely," he said, stepping back so she could enter. "Can I help?"

She laughed while she greeted Boomer. "Mom got her notebook out and the conversation was getting intense. I was trying to sneak away for a shower when I heard 'we need to make a list' and I'm not proud of it, but I threw some stuff in a bag and ran."

"That paint's been in your hair awhile. You might need some help washing it out, and I'm happy to volunteer for the job."

She gave Boomer a final pat and turned back to Case, hauling him in for a sizzling kiss that had him moaning against her mouth. "I kind of thought you might."

After giving Boomer a fresh dog chew to demolish and putting a baseball game on for him, Case grabbed her bag and led her up the stairs.

It didn't take long for Gwen to realize Case's fingers gently working shampoo through her hair while his naked body pressed against hers was one of her new favorite things. When he found a clump of paint, he'd work it with his fingers until it broke up and could be washed away. And he even managed to stay focused while she was running her hands over his slick body.

She couldn't help herself. She loved the feel of his lean muscles under her hands, and if she didn't explore him thoroughly, how would she know he had a ticklish spot halfway up his right side?

"I think I got it all," he said, sliding his lathered hands down her back. "And as much as I really, really want to have fun shower sex with you, this is an old house and we'll be lucky if the hot water holds out long enough to rinse us both off."

Her disappointment only lasted until he wrapped her in a soft, oversize towel. He was *very* thorough in drying her off—running his hands over the skin he'd dried to make sure he hadn't missed a spot. Blowing softly across her nipples, and stroking the sensitive flesh between her thighs with his hand instead of the towel.

He was so thorough, she was practically whimpering by the time he tossed the towel on the floor and backed her up to the bed. Gwen buried her fingers in the damp hair at the back of his neck and kissed him, taking him with her as she fell back on the mattress.

Case lifted her against his body, not breaking off the kiss as he shifted them into the bed. His teeth caught her bottom lip as he brushed his thumb across her taut nipple, and she couldn't help smiling against his mouth. She loved the sensation of his work-hardened hands against her soft flesh.

When he finally moved between her thighs and slowly pushed into her body—his gaze locked with hers—it was as if a sigh passed through her. Not just of pleasure, but of how *right* it all felt. Luckily, he closed his eyes as he thrust fully into her and then dropped his head to nip at her jawline and her neck, so he didn't see the sudden sheen of threatening tears she had to blink away.

Then the shadows of giving this—of giving *him*—up were chased away by delicious sensations as he rocked his hips, harder and faster with each thrust.

She scraped her fingernails down his back, running her hands over the curve of his ass, and then moaned when he caught her nipple in his mouth and sucked hard. When he reached between them to stroke her clit, she arched her back as her hands gripped his upper arms.

The orgasm built until she had to bite down on her lip to keep from calling out his name, and she'd barely caught her breath before he groaned, his body jerking against hers as he found his release. He collapsed on top of her, and she wrapped her legs around his hips to hold him close as his breath came in hot gusts against her neck.

After a moment, he had to dispose of the condom, but then he pulled her against his body. He kissed her hair and her jaw and her mouth before settling with his arm across her. It wasn't until she tried to shift and had to lift her head to free her hair that she realized what had been freshly washed hair was probably now a tangled, rapidly drying mess.

She sighed, partly in contentment and partly from

the knowledge she couldn't stay like this. "I don't want to get up."

"Then don't," he murmured against her shoulder.

"If my hair dries like this, I might have to shave my head in the morning." As it was, she'd have her work cut out for her.

She smiled when he just made a sleepy sound of amusement and pulled her closer. As much as she wanted to close her eyes and drift off to sleep, she didn't. She hadn't been kidding about her hair, but maybe she could wait a few more minutes.

It was still light enough so she could look around his bedroom, and she smiled when she saw the sweaters draped on the back of the chair. They'd probably been there awhile, seeing as how it was the end of July.

The end of July.

The familiar pang of panic struck and she squeezed her eyes closed. In a few days, it would be August and not only would she still be here in Stonefield, but they didn't even have a date for the brewery to open yet.

Now wasn't the time to stress about her book and needing to have at least an idea of when she could go back to the comfortable writing haven she'd made for herself in Vermont. Not when she was sated and comfortable, with the weight of Case's arm across her body. She couldn't help it, though.

Only now when she thought about going home, it got tangled up with having to leave Case. Inevitable as it was, she knew it was still going to hurt.

"Can I ask you a personal question?" she asked without thinking.

"I'm not sure what's considered a personal question when you're naked in bed together," he said, running his hand over her hip. "I also think that question becomes kind of unnecessary once people have showered together."

She smiled and gave a little shrug. "Good point. But it's one of those questions that's hard to phrase the right way, you know?"

"You should just ask it and then I'll know."

"Do you still live in this house because you *want* to, or because it was your parents' house?" She didn't bother to add the part about how it had passed to him when he lost both of his parents—his mother from cancer and his father from a stroke not even two years later—because it was somewhat implied in the question.

"Are you asking if I live here because I didn't have to buy it, or because I can't let go of something that belonged to my mom and dad on an emotional level?"

She fought the need to squirm, but when he looked at her, she could see that he wasn't offended by the question. He was simply trying to clarify what she was asking. "Let me try it this way—if you did sell this house, what kind of house would you buy for *yourself*?"

He thought about it, but only for a few seconds. "This one."

She laughed, shaking her head. "I guess that answers that."

"It's a great house in a great neighborhood. Plenty of yard for my dog. Rooms for the kids I'll have, hopefully someday soon. A garage for my truck if I ever clean all the other crap out of it. I live across from the hottest woman in town. Why would I want to live anywhere else?"

Rooms for the kids I'll have, hopefully someday soon.

It took everything she had to keep her smile from slipping. This was a man with a plan, and that plan included spending the rest of his life in Stonefield—in this very house, actually. She'd guessed that, of course. But hearing the confirmation he'd never even considered leaving this town come from his very own mouth was a bit of a blow.

And the *hopefully someday soon* just kept echoing around in her head. Mallory had been right. Case was ready to settle down. He wanted to start a family and not just someday, but someday *soon.* And he wanted that family to live in this house—the house he'd grown up in. She couldn't let herself forget that.

Over the next two weeks, Gwen crossed the street to visit Case almost every night, though she always went home before his bedtime. He got up *very* early and she definitely did not. And she didn't want him staying up late, either, because he had a dangerous job and he needed to be able to focus on what he was doing.

But the evenings belonged to them. They'd watch television, and play with Boomer in the backyard. One night they'd forgone their time in bed to take the dog back to the river, and she hadn't minded at all. While she definitely liked having Case in bed, she liked spending time with him outside of the bedroom, too.

Much to her surprise, neither her mother nor her sisters had said a word. Oh, there were speculative looks and a few knowing smiles, especially from her mother, but they kept their opinions about it to themselves. As much as she'd like to think they were actually minding their own business, she knew better. They didn't want to push too hard and have her pull back from Case.

She didn't care why. All she cared about was them leaving her alone and giving her that space. She and Case knew there was no pressure, like he'd said. They were enjoying each other's company. And they were enjoying it a *lot*.

That was all that mattered.

Shortly after he got home from work on a Thursday that felt like a Monday, Case was surprised to look out his window and see that Lane sitting in a rocker on his front porch was the reason for Boomer's excited woofing sounds. He was even more surprised to see a fat three-ring binder on his cousin's lap. A small bottle of Captain Morgan was sitting on the table beside him.

He wasn't sure what was up, but he knew how to do his part. After splitting ice and a can of cola between two glasses, he opened the door and joined Lane on the porch. While Boomer greeted his other favorite person, Case added some spiced rum to each of the glasses and settled into his rocker.

"Are we celebrating or commiserating?" he asked after taking a cautious sip—yes, another accidental strong pour. He rarely made mixed drinks and wasn't very good at judging how much alcohol to add, so it was a good thing they usually stuck to beer. He should probably never get roped into playing bartender at the tavern if they ever added mixed drinks, either. Happy customers, but not so happy alcohol budget.

"Celebrating," Lane said as Boomer sprawled at his feet, ready to resume his predinner nap so he'd be well rested for the postdinner nap he had to fit in before bedtime. "I have more certificates and stamps and signatures and permits than I know what to do with, but all of our i's are dotted and our t's are crossed. Sutton's Place Brewery & Tavern is officially allowed to open."

"Congratulations," he said, reaching over so they could clink glasses. That explained the rum. Knowing a bureaucratic hiccup could keep them from opening the doors despite all the time and money— to say nothing of plain old hard work—they'd sunk into it had to have been hard on the nerves.

"Thanks. I just left the town hall with the last piece of the puzzle."

"And you're not letting it out of your sight?" Case asked, gesturing at the binder on Lane's lap.

"Nope. I'm keeping my hands on this stuff until it's home and in the safe."

"Have you told them yet?" Case asked, nodding his head toward the house across the street.

"Not yet. I will, but today's Evie's birthday, and they're doing a family dinner and cake thing. I'm surprised you didn't get invited."

They couldn't really invite Case without inviting Lane, so keeping it strictly family was the easiest way to get around Evie's ex-husband being at her birthday party, but Case didn't feel a need to say that out loud. "This news would add to the celebration."

"I know Ellen's been worried about it, but I know their relief will be short-lived and give way to a million more things that need to be talked about or done, so I'll let Evie have her cake in peace. And getting through all this paperwork and red tape is the hardest thing I've ever accomplished, and right now, I just want to relax and enjoy it." Lane snorted and gave a quick shake of his head. "I might even sleep tonight."

He did look the most relaxed he'd been in so many months, Case couldn't even count them, he thought. And it wasn't just in the lines of his face. Lane's entire body was less tense, and it wouldn't have surprised Case any if his cousin didn't even wait to get home to sleep, but just nodded off in the rocking chair. If he made a second round of drinks, there wouldn't be any doubt about it.

"Besides a celebratory drink," Lane said, "I wanted to stop here so I could say thank you. I know I don't say it enough—hell, I don't know if I've said it *at all*—but I'm aware this hasn't been easy on you, and I appreciate that you've taken on so much to help make this happen for me."

Case almost waved off the gratitude as unnecessary, but it was actually nice to hear Lane acknowledge it. "Thanks. Some days it's tough, but we're going to get through it. The tree service was chosen *for* us, and I'm okay with that, but I'm not going to begrudge you wanting to do something else."

"That's just it, though. I don't want to walk away from the company. I know it would probably be easier if I did because then you could straight up replace me, but I want to cut trees *and* brew beer." He waved a hand toward the carriage house—which they should probably start calling the tavern all the time, but old habits were hard to break. "It's all the rest of it that's necessary to support the brewing that's a pain in the ass."

"At some point, that'll all be settled. Eventually there's going to be staff to handle all the rest of it, so you can cut trees and brew beer. That's probably close to a year down the road, but we'll all make some sacrifices and do some compromising and get through it."

Lane gave him a long, somber look. "Just promise me that if you get near a breaking point, you'll tell me so I can make adjustments before it blows up. I don't want this to come between you and me."

"I'll say something, because I don't want it to, either. And it won't." He took another sip of his drink, managing not to wince this time. "And since we're talking about feelings, what's going on with you and Evie? It's obvious things have settled for you since Old Home Day, but not quite all the way."

Lane shrugged. "That day we ended up crossing paths behind the fire department's booth, which has had that huge wooden truck ever since the year there was a fire and the real truck had to plow through evacuated booths to get out. We had our first kiss behind that booth and we were laughing about it and then...yeah. Things were getting heated and we went with hot tempers instead of a hot kiss."

"And since then?"

"Pretending it didn't almost happen. Trying to keep busy. We haven't been alone together since, which is for the best." He took a long swallow of his drink and Case noticed his cousin didn't wince at all. "As much as having Gwen and Evie home has helped, it would be a hell of a lot easier on me if Evie moved on to wherever she's going to next."

Case tried to focus on Evie, but thinking about her leaving made him think about Gwen leaving, so he strongly disagreed with that sentiment in a knee-jerk kind of way. But he knew having his ex-wife not only back in town, but a part of his everyday life, thanks to the brewery, was really hard on Lane.

"Speaking of Gwen," Lane said, "I'm not keeping you from anything, am I?"

"Not at all. She said she might come over later, or

she might try to write some, depending on what was going on at the house. She didn't mention it being Evie's birthday, so they obviously wanted to keep all the cake to themselves." He shrugged. "But there's no reason you being here is a problem, anyway. She'd be happy to drink a toast to your paperwork win."

"You might want to let me make the drink, though." Lane chuckled. "This drink was so strong, you should feed me supper before you let me go home."

"It wasn't *that* strong. I'm more than happy to throw an extra steak on the grill, but my excellent mixology skills aren't the reason." They both laughed, and Case shook his head. "My first thought when I tasted it was that you'd go bankrupt fast if you served mixed drinks and let me tend bar."

"We don't need a bartender," Lane said, the amusement gone. "That's Evie's job."

"Only for now," Case reminded him.

It was a state of being he was pretty familiar with. Gwen was in town—for now. They were enjoying each other's company in *and* out of bed—for now. Life was good and Case was happier than he'd been in a long time.

For now.

Chapter Sixteen

Great news, Stonefield! Mark your calendars, because the official grand opening date for Sutton's Place Brewery & Tavern is Friday, September 10th! They'll add Thursday night to the schedule the following week, but all the best parties are on Friday nights! We'll see you there!

—Stonefield Gazette *Facebook Page*

Once the paperwork and permits were all in order and Sutton's Place was officially a go, everything kicked into a high gear that left Gwen exhausted at the end of every day. When she finally closed the door of her bedroom every evening, she was too physically and mentally exhausted to even open her laptop. Her own workday had been whittled down to cursory checks of her email before she went to bed. Everybody's focus was on the brewery now, and getting ready to serve Lane's concoctions to their friends and family.

And it was about time. She had no idea what Lane was actually doing in that cellar, but it had meant a lot to her dad and it was time to share it. Whenever Lane talked about it, it sounded to her as if he was conducting a giant science experiment and there were a lot of words and phrases she didn't recognize.

This had been her father's passion, she thought sadly, and she didn't know a thing about it. Sure, she'd heard him talk about beer a lot and he'd shown her a few of the recipes and equipment sketches in his notebook, but in her experience, beer was a thing a *lot* of men talked about. But she didn't think the majority of men who were less than ten years from retirement mortgaged everything to brew their own.

But that line of thinking only stirred up the painful mix of sorrow, loss, resentment and even anger, so she took a deep breath. She was never going to understand why her dad had chosen to do this. All she could do was accept it and do her best to help her mom make it happen.

Right now, helping Mom meant making a massive bowl of salad to go with the chicken and potatoes that Mallory was cooking on the grill. Ellen was upstairs, off her feet for a little while, and Evie was setting the table. As soon as Lane and Case came in from hanging the last of the trim that Gwen and Evie had stained yesterday, they'd eat. It was Mallory who'd made the executive decision to eat inside—in the air-conditioning—rather than in the gazebo.

And when they were done eating, they'd be back out in the carriage house. With the trim and lighting all up, it was time for the guys to carry in the tables and stools from where they'd been stored with the grain. And the women would be setting up the bar area. It was starting to come together fast now, but with only four weeks between the final piece of the paperwork puzzle and opening their doors, sometimes it didn't feel fast enough.

Her mom walked in, looking slightly refreshed, to see how the dinner preparations were going. "That salad looks good. And I just adjusted that thermo-stat. Keeping it cool is one thing, but unless we're expecting penguins for dinner, it doesn't need to be *this* cool. The electric bill's going to be painful."

"What else is new?"

Ellen paused, frowning. "What do you mean?"

"The utilities are always painful because this house costs a crap ton of money to cool and to heat, and just think of all the time you spend cleaning. You don't need all these rooms."

"I need the carriage house, though, since we're about to open a business in it. And of course I need the rooms. You're here, and Evie. Not only would Mallory and I having separate homes probably cost us more in the long run, where would you and your sister sleep if I had a small place?"

"Lord only knows where Evie would sleep, but I'd sleep in my own bedroom, in the house in Vermont I actually live in." When her mom frowned, Gwen's stomach knotted. Though she kept her voice as soft as possible, she didn't want her mom getting her hopes up about Gwen staying. "Me being here is temporary, Mom. You know that because I've been very up-front about it since the day I got here. I was willing to stay until the beginning of August and now it'll be mid-September and I didn't want to stay this long."

"But things have changed since then."

Understanding dropped on Gwen like a granite block—her mother was talking about Case. Somehow the woman had gotten it into her head that Gwen wasn't going to leave Stonefield because her feelings for a man were going to keep her in town. And she did have feelings for a man, but she wasn't blowing up her career for him. "Nothing has changed, Mom."

"We'll see."

Gwen's eyes widened, but she kept herself from opening her mouth until she had a better idea of what might come out of it. The only thing they were going to see was her taillights when she drove out of town after this brewery business was sorted out. But, she reminded herself, she'd made that resolution about being more careful about what she said to her mother. She didn't want to break it now.

Unfortunately she couldn't come up with a rebuttal that didn't sound outraged or snarky in her head, so she kept her mouth shut. Luckily, she heard Mallory and the guys coming inside, so it was time to eat, anyway.

As always, dinner became a business meeting. They talked so much about Sutton's Place that Mallory had at some point relaxed the dinner rules for Jack and Eli, and the boys ate in the living room with the TV on because it was better company.

"Have you guys settled on the hours yet?" Case asked almost as soon as he'd fixed his plate.

"We think it's best to be open Thursday through Sunday for now, from three o'clock to ten o'clock, and eight on Sundays. I'll have to close the shop at two on those days, but people will get used to it."

"You'll only have an hour between closing the thrift shop and opening the taproom," Gwen pointed out.

"I think Mallory will probably leave the thrift shop earlier, and I'll close it up. Eventually we'll probably go back to regular hours at Sutton's Seconds, but I think for at least a few weeks, we'll have one at a time open."

The rest of them talked all through the meal, but Gwen didn't give them her full attention. Her mind was still on the conversation with her mom in the kitchen. On some level, she'd been afraid her mom would get her hopes up about Case and Gwen's relationship being serious enough to keep her in Stone-field, but having her fear confirmed was unsettling.

When they were finished, but before anybody got up from their seats, Evie spoke. "I have something I want to show you before we go back to work."

She retrieved a box Gwen hadn't noticed from the dining room and brought it back to set on the kitchen table. When she opened it and took out one of the glasses they'd ordered, everybody looked confused.

"Most of the boxes are in the taproom since we're doing the glasses this week, but I took a few of them to try something." She held up a glass with the Sutton's Place logo on it. "There's one for each of us."

When she'd passed them all out, Gwen realized Evie had etched their names into the glass. In a clean, bold script, the *Gwen* was subtle but visible under the logo. It looked nice, and she told her sister so.

"Thanks," Evie said after everybody had complimented their glasses. "But they're not just keepsakes. So hear me out before you react. People like to be a part of things—to belong to something. Like the guys who have their regular seats at the coffee counter at the diner. Or how the knitting club gets the comfy seats at the library on Tuesday nights. They not only visit these places, but they have a sense of belonging there. I think when a person becomes a regular at Sutton's Place, they get their own glass with their name etched on it. There can be a special shelf for those glasses, and when that customer comes in, he or she gets that feeling of being part of it."

She paused and reached into the box to pull out another glass, which she set in the middle of the table. Gwen had to lean forward to read it, and then tears blurred her vision and she had to blink them away.

David. Cheers, until we meet again.

It was Case who got up to go in search of a box of tissues, since the tears were pretty immediate.

Gwen's eyes were dry, though, as she stared at the glass in her hands, replaying Evie's words about being a part of something and belonging in her mind. And they made the glass feel as if it weighed about a hundred pounds. She didn't think it was deliberate on Evie's part—she couldn't very well make a glass for all of them and leave Gwen out—but she couldn't help feeling there was some kind of subliminal message in it.

You belong at Sutton's Place.

But she didn't. She'd always be a part of it, of course. It was a family business. But she intended to be a part of it from a distance. Actually belonging was a different story. She belonged in Vermont, finishing her book and then going for quiet, solitary walks to plan the next one.

Case's knee bumped hers as he sat back down, and she looked sideways to find him smiling at her. When his leg stretched out along the length of hers, warm and firm, she smiled back. His glass was on the table and she watched as he took hers out of her hand and set it next to his.

Gwen. Case.

Side-by-side. Belonging.

To her dismay, tears welled up in her eyes, and she could only hope anybody who noticed—especially Case—would blame the emotion that had overwhelmed the room when Evie showed them their father's glass.

But those tears had come with the realization that she was in over her head with Case. She was falling in love with him, and every day they spent together, she fell a little bit more. And that meant that every day she spent in Stonefield was going to make it that much harder to leave him. There might even come a time when she surrendered to spending the rest of her life in this town, going back to writing bits of books when she got a chance and she'd worked too hard building her career to even wrap her head around that.

It was time to go home.

Something had changed in Gwen when the glasses came out. Case couldn't quite put his finger on it or define what it was, but something was definitely going on with her. He didn't have to wait long for the answer to his unspoken question, though. Once they'd all agreed to embrace the etched glasses, they were talking about who was doing what for the grand opening when she dropped the news.

"We should probably talk about this in the context of me not really being a part of it," Gwen said quietly during a break in the conversation. "So we can make sure everything runs okay, I mean. I'll be here for the grand opening to help out if needed, but then I'm going home. To Vermont."

Case froze, not wanting to give away the impact her words had on him. That impact was how he imagined it would feel to have a wrecking ball come out of nowhere and drive into him, knocking him off a cliff into a river that tumbled him against rocks until he slammed into a massive concrete dam.

It hurt, to say the least.

She was leaving. And not only was she leaving, but she was leaving *soon* and she hadn't even bothered to talk to him about it. To tell him first, privately, rather than blowing his life apart without warning and in front of her entire family.

"So soon?" Ellen asked when the silence had stretched past awkward and into downright painful.

"Soon? Mom, I've been here for almost three months and we're not even open yet. You knew it was temporary and, to be honest, I feel like once the bar is open, it's going to be too easy for everybody to keep assuming I'll just be here the next day to work, and the day after that. The grand opening feels like a segue into a new phase, and I'm not going to be here for that phase. I can't write here and they've already given me two extensions. If I miss my new deadline, I… I just can't."

Case heard the conversation, but the words swirled around in his head in a way he couldn't make sense of. He wasn't grasping what she said in a logical way, but rather was *feeling* her words as emotions that pummeled his senses.

There was still nothing in Stonefield she wanted to stay in town for.

When everybody got up to leave the table, he was slow to do the same. Ellen and Gwen were still bickering about her departure as they walked away with their hands full of dinner dishes—Mallory and Evie right behind them. He knew he should grab some dishes and follow, but his feet didn't move.

Actually, they did want to move. They wanted to carry him out the door and across the street to his house, where he could be alone to process the news his heart was going to be broken sooner rather than later.

But he still had furniture to move, and as much as he wanted to be alone, he couldn't let Lane down.

"We can do this another night," his cousin said, as if he could read his mind.

"No." Case tried to shake it off. "Tomorrow night's not going to be any better than tonight. Let's just get it done."

They worked until it was almost time for Case to be in bed, Boomer watching from the doorway of the taproom with his head propped on his front paws. He'd been with Jack and Eli until Mallory called it a night to get them to bed, and Ellen had gone in at the same time. Rather than go home alone, he was waiting for his person.

But as soon as the tables and stools had been placed and rearranged several times until everybody was happy with the placement, Case was done. "That's it for me. Five-thirty comes early."

"Thanks for helping," Gwen said, her eyes on him.

"Not a problem. I'll see you all tomorrow after work."

Just before he turned to leave, he saw the flash of hurt across her face, but he didn't stop and try to make it better. He *couldn't* make it better. And as he walked out, Boomer at his side, he couldn't make sense of why she should be hurt at all. She hadn't even brought up the possibility of visiting each other—of continuing on even after she went back to Vermont, until they could figure out what they wanted. No pressure, he thought. Just enjoying each other's company.

But if their relationship wasn't important enough to her to merit a conversation about her leaving before she announced it at the dinner table as a done deal, then it wasn't important enough to be sad about.

The next two weeks were as bad as that night. The only bright spot was all of them taking a break to watch Jack and Eli race their derby cars at summer camp, where the pain of watching Gwen laugh with her family and nephews was almost too much. Otherwise, he worked his ass off all day and then helped out at the tavern at night. His time over there was coming to an end, though. The heavy lifting was done. All the historical brewing items and memorabilia David had collected over his lifetime had been displayed.

The paving company finished the parking lot, so he and Lane had fixed the landscaping that was impacted by the work. They'd mounted the Sutton's Place Brewery & Tavern sign on a granite pillar.

They were down to the final touches, with Lane focusing on the brewing and the Sutton women finishing the kitchen and stocking the food they'd need, while Mallory also juggled the boys going back to school. They didn't need him for any of that, so he started spending more time keeping Jack and Eli busy in the yard with Boomer in the evenings.

Gwen hadn't been over since the night Evie revealed the glasses. Case wasn't sure if it was because everything had changed between them that night, or if it was just a case of being so tired she just went to bed early, but it was a hard adjustment.

He already missed her and she hadn't even left yet.

Chapter Seventeen

Tonight is the grand opening of Sutton's Place Brewery & Tavern! Stop by and see how they've transformed the carriage house into a taproom, drink some beer and raise a glass to David Sutton! Ellen and her daughters, along with Lane Thompson and Case Danforth, have worked hard, so let's show them some support. And don't forget that Stonefield House of Pizza will deliver to the brewery, so let's eat, drink (responsibly) and be merry!

—Stonefield Gazette *Facebook Page*

"Is it a bad look if we close early the first night we're open?" Mallory asked in a low voice, so nobody else could hear.

Gwen laughed, feeling almost as exhausted as her sister sounded. Mallory might be used to being on the move—what with working at the thrift shop all day and having two young boys—but Gwen's days used to be about desk chairs and comfortable recliners. She wasn't accustomed to being on her feet like this.

Ellen stood in the middle of the taproom and did a slow turn, giving everything a final once-over. Gwen tried not to roll her eyes, but they'd gone over everything so often she could probably describe every aspect of the brewery with her eyes closed. They'd made a few adjustments about who was doing what, though.

Tonight Gwen would be floating to wherever needed, if she was needed at all. They'd finally taken her seriously when she told them to plan around her, and the only specific task assigned to her was keeping the popcorn machine they'd bought after Old Home Day popping. And Mallory had put her foot down. Her boys going with the flow and enjoying some relaxed rules over the summer was one thing, but they were back in school and needed structured meals, homework time and bedtime. She would rather be with them herself, but she knew that wasn't practical. She was, however, adamant that their grandmother be with them in the house.

Even though they were still hoping not to hire anybody until closer to the end of the year, Ellen had looked visibly relieved when Mallory made that declaration. Taking care of her grandsons would be a lot easier on her after a day at the thrift store than being on her feet in the tavern. But they'd had to let Lane know in no uncertain terms that brewing the beer was his primary job, but he was going to pull his weight upstairs, too.

For tonight, though, Mallory had hired a sitter and it was all hands on deck.

Mallory was going to run the kitchen, while Evie took care of the tables and helped Lane behind the bar. They all knew Ellen would spend most of the night talking to their customers. It wasn't ideal, but it should be sustainable for the three of them. They just didn't sit that many people at a time.

Right now, though, there was chaos. Gwen ran up the stairs to the storage area to grab a box of napkins, and almost ran into Case. A box fell out of his arms as he reached out to steady her and, just like that, she was in his arms. He tightened them around her and pressed his cheek to the top of her head, and she breathed in the scent of him.

Her fingers pressed into his back, holding him close to her, and when she spoke, her voice was muffled by his chest. "I've missed you."

"I've missed you, too."

"Everything has been so out of control and I'm so tired."

"I know." He pressed a kiss to the spot his cheek had been and then rested his chin on her head. "Everybody's tired. But once it's open, everybody will find a rhythm and relax."

"I hope so." She straightened, pulling away from him even though she was reluctant to let go. Her body ached with a need to stay close to him, but giving in wasn't going to make leaving any easier. "I have to get another box of napkins downstairs."

He nodded and moved back so he could pick up the box he'd dropped. The tension in his eyes and his body language tore at her heart, but she couldn't allow herself to try to soothe it. There was no way to fix it. But she'd only gone a few steps toward the boxes of napkins when he said her name and she turned. "Maybe after the grand opening, we can talk."

She smiled and nodded. She really didn't want to leave Stonefield with tension between them, and no matter how much it would hurt, they needed a proper goodbye. "I'd like that."

The final few minutes before they opened the doors was hectic enough to require almost all of her attention, but every time her gaze landed on Case, her heart hurt just a little bit more.

"Are we ready?" Ellen asked, and they all nodded. There were already several people outside, and Gwen didn't want them changing their minds. "Okay. This is it."

It went beautifully. Gwen knew all the planning and the work and the endless discussions had been worth it before the first hour they were open was up. Granted, the customers were friends, but it was Stonefield. Word would spread.

She saw Laura and Daphne in the crowd. Molly and her parents. So many people she knew—had known most of her life, if not all of it—as well as a few people she didn't recognize.

Case was there, too. He mingled, table-hopping to talk to the people he knew—which was everybody—but judging by how often she caught him watching her, she knew he never lost track of what she was doing.

She'd told him they'd talk after the grand opening, and every time their eyes locked across the taproom, she was so overcome by emotion, she had to look away. Saying goodbye to him was going to hurt like hell.

But she had to go home. She couldn't risk her book being pulled from the publisher's schedule. She'd worked too hard to build a reputation with her readers.

"Can you take over for a minute?" Lane asked her when she stepped behind the bar on her way to the kitchen.

"Sure." It wasn't hard, and he'd made all of them practice with the taps until they could get a perfect pour with just the right amount of foam. "You look nervous."

"I am."

"The beer is good, Lane. You have nothing to be nervous about."

He made a noncommittal sound and then gave her a considering look. "Maybe you, of all the people here, should understand it, though. You put everything into writing a book. You think it's good, and the people around you tell you it's good. But those people care about *you*, so you probably get nervous when it's time for it to hit the bookstores."

He certainly wasn't wrong about that. "I've got this if you want to take a break."

"I just need a second."

She thought he'd head for the men's room, but he just turned, poured himself a glass of water and headed away from the bar. He looked like he was psyching himself up for something, and she really hoped he wasn't on the verge of a breakdown. They could work around the rest of the family, but they couldn't have a brewery without Lane.

But after a moment to compose himself, he turned back to face the taproom and yelled over the crowd. "Can I have everybody's attention for a minute?"

It took a moment for the crowd to quiet, but soon all eyes were on Lane. And he didn't look happy about it. Gwen saw the slight bead of sweat on his brow and knew he'd love more than anything to run into his cellar and not come out for a while.

Ellen moved to stand next to Gwen, and she saw Evie and Mallory come from the kitchen to listen as Lane started to talk.

"David and I talked about this brewery for years. Honestly, I'm not sure either of us ever intended to actually do it, but we were in the carriage house one day and we started playing a serious game of *what if* and, well, this is the culmination of a whole lot of what ifs." He paused and then cleared his throat, which sounded harsh in the quiet taproom. "I say that so you know that when I tell you David talked to me for years about brewing, I mean *years.*"

Ellen chuckled. "I was always thankful he had you, Lane, so I didn't have to listen to him go on about it."

Amusement rippled through the room and the warm affection and remembered exasperation glowing on her mother's face made Gwen smile. She'd been so afraid this night would magnify their sense of loss—that they'd all be hyperaware that her dad was missing—but instead, sitting here, surrounded by his dream and the people who loved him the most, she could almost feel his arms wrapped around her in a fierce dad hug.

"You all know how important this brewery was to David," Lane continued, "but there was more to it."

When he pulled a thick, leather-bound journal from the shelf under the bar and set it on top of the polished wood, emotion knotted in Gwen's throat. There it was, the pages swollen from years of being flipped through and written on with her father's heavy hand. The leather binding the paper had a gorgeous patina from age and use, and her fingers itched to touch it.

"David experimented a lot over the years, brewing some incredible brews and some really, really bad beer." Lane had to stop for laughter again, and Gwen could see that he was bracing himself somehow, as if he had a hard part to get through. "It was important to him that we launch this brewery with three distinct, exceptional beers—each one an expression of love for his three daughters."

Oh, they were going to need tissues, Gwen thought, but she was unable to move. So that's why there were four taps, but he'd only allowed them to use one. She knew the beer they'd toasted the name with was the same one they'd been serving tonight, and she'd had no idea there were more.

"You've been drinking our house lager tonight," Lane announced. "But we're going to offer everybody samples of the three beers I'm about to introduce."

Mallory and Evie had come forward to stand with Ellen and Gwen, and Mallory whispered to their mother, "Did you know about this?"

Ellen shook her head, pressing the napkin Evie had slipped into her hand against her mouth. Gwen and Evie both shook their heads, too, even though she hadn't asked them.

"I'm not going to say a lot about each one," Lane said. "I'm just going to tell you what was underlined and circled and highlighted in his journal. The rest of the notes, his daughters can read privately."

Then he picked up one of the smaller glasses he'd insisted they get for flights, even though they'd argued it didn't make sense to have flights when they only had a lager. He poured the first, a very dark, almost black beer that made several people in the crowd make noises of appreciation.

"Gwen." He glanced at her and gave her a smile before looking down at the journal. "American Imperial Stout. Strong. Might be too much for some people, but is perfect for the right people."

She didn't even try to stop the tears flowing down her cheeks. Her dad had been one of those right people because he'd never made her feel anything less than unconditionally loved, just the way she was.

The next pour was a rich golden color. "American wheat beer for Mallory. Light. Pairs well with anything. Can bring things together, like my Mal. And finally…"

He paused before the final pour, which was also golden, but much lighter than the second. Gwen, whose hands were being squeezed by Evie and her mother watched his jaw clench, and she knew he was trying not to look emotional while sharing his former father-in-law's snapshot of Evie.

"Evie," he said, and he locked gazes with her for a few seconds before clearing his throat. "Bright and citrusy and refreshing. Mood lifting."

He paused as applause swelled in the room and the Sutton women went through a stack of bar napkins trying to stop the tears. Even Lane looked emotional, and Gwen's heart ached for him. Sometimes it was easy to forget that he hadn't just been her dad's business partner, but his codreamer for many years. And like Ellen, Lane was having to cherish this dream without the man he'd shared it with.

"You might have noticed the beers don't have names," Lane said finally, his voice raised to be heard again. "I'm not creative that way and David hadn't named them yet. His notes as he worked on the brewing process for these were only cataloged under the women's names and…well, there's one final note I'll read to you. 'I can't call them by the girls' names because if some guy comes in and says he's in the mood for some Mallory tonight, I'll have to knock him out, and that's bad for business.'"

The laughter that rippled through the crowd was the perfect note to end on, so Lane closed the journal and brought it to Ellen. "Thank you for lending this to me. I know it's special, but I wanted the beers to be perfect for him. And for them, too, so I needed his notes."

Gwen watched her mother stroke the worn leather cover, another tear sliding over her cheek, and she wasn't surprised when Ellen pressed it back into his hands. "You keep this, Lane. You shared this with him in a way we never could and I want you to have it."

There was a moment when Gwen wanted to go and snatch it out of Lane's hands. It was filled with her father's handwriting—with years of his dreams—but she fought the urge. They were dreams he'd shared with Lane, and Lane was the primary reason they'd made it happen. She knew that book meant as much to him as it did to her and her sisters.

He kissed her cheek and then blew out a deep breath. "Thank you, but it doesn't belong to me."

Ellen smiled. "It belongs to all of us—to this place."

"We'll keep it with his other treasures, then," Lane said, nodding toward the display behind the glass doors, and then he smiled back at her. "Now, let's pour some beer."

In a blind taste test, Case probably would have picked the pale ale, but Gwen had her eye on him. And when he'd chosen the stout, she'd given him one of those smiles that lit up her face, so as far as he was concerned, it was his new favorite drink.

Luckily, the tears had passed, and everybody was in high spirits again. He sat with Daphne for a while, listening to her tell a story about an Oktoberfest in the '80s he would rather not have heard.

He saw a lot of people eating, and it looked like the partnership with S-HoP was going well. But he'd make a point to tell Ellen they didn't want to run the kid doing the deliveries too much. Maybe a one order per group rule. One table had wanted wings, but then they wanted a pizza, too, and then they called in to see if desserts were available.

Smiling to himself, he realized he was going to be more of a part of this than he'd originally intended. Even though he was here strictly as a customer, he couldn't stop watching for things they'd done really right or things they could improve on.

Then he heard Ellen's voice, saying words that destroyed the evening instantly.

"She's leaving tomorrow, probably late morning, so she'll be back in Vermont before we reopen tomorrow. I know now that we can do this without her, but I'll miss having her around."

Case realized he'd stopped walking and was just standing near a table in the taproom, so he forced himself to keep walking. There was no reason he couldn't leave, but he'd gone in the direction of the bar on autopilot. He leaned on it, setting down the almost empty glass of porter.

"Want another?"

Of course it had to be Gwen. When he looked up, shaking his head, Lane was nowhere in sight. Great time to take a break, he thought. "No, I'm good."

After looking at him for a few seconds, her brow furrowed. "You don't look like you're good. What's wrong? And please don't say food poisoning."

Her attempt at a joke fell flat between them. He was too numb to fake it. "I just overheard Ellen telling her friends you're leaving tomorrow and how much she's going to miss having you around."

"I know she'll miss me. She keeps telling me that."

"Tomorrow, Gwen?" He couldn't keep the hurt out of his voice. There was too much of it.

She paused, giving him her full attention. "You were there when I said I was leaving after the grand opening."

"I didn't realize you meant the very next day. Like, after the grand opening, *period*. Maybe because we haven't talked about it. Not the whole group, but just you and me."

"I said we could talk tonight, after we close. To say goodbye." She closed her eyes for a moment, maybe to block out the pain on his face that he couldn't hide. "Case, you always knew I was leaving. You said we were enjoying each other's company. No pressure."

"That was—" He bit back the word *before*. Before he fell completely in love with her. Before he started imagining they might have a life together. He knew she had to go back to Vermont, at least for a little while. But she lived two hours away. They could juggle some long-distance stuff. She could finish her book. They'd figure it out. But it didn't appear any of that was a part of *her* plan.

She flinched, hurt crossing her face. "Do we have to do this right now? I'm a little busy."

He shrugged, a casual gesture meant to disguise how much he was hurting on the inside. "We don't have to do it at all. It is what it is, and we both knew that's *all* it was."

He walked out, not bothering to say goodbye to anybody. They were all busy, and he didn't have it in him to act like everything was okay, even for a few minutes. Instead he went home and greeted his dog, who followed him around the house sniffing at his legs, trying to figure out who he'd been with.

Two hours later, Gwen's light went on. He knew because he was standing at the window, staring at her bedroom and trying to figure out how things had gotten so out of control between them.

He still believed if things calmed down—if the two of them could escape the situation for even a few days—they could work it out. And that's why he took the cap off the Sharpie and scrawled one word across a piece of poster board.

Stay.

He saw movement in her window—her shape blocking the light—and then she was gone. But a minute later, her whiteboard appeared.

I can't. Go with me.

The invitation hit him like a fist to the chest, bruising his heart. Gwen wanted him to go with her to Vermont. She wanted him. She just didn't want him *here*.

Happiness swelled in him, but it was like a roller coaster reaching the top of a steep climb. A moment of relief and happiness, and then came the drop. But his roller coaster didn't just drop. It plummeted and went off the rails.

He didn't really know anything about where Gwen lived, except that it was a condo. Even if they allowed dogs, he didn't think Boomer would like condo living. And Case owned his home. He wasn't opposed to selling it, even though it had belonged to his parents, but he liked it. It suited him, as did everything about his life in Stonefield.

But there was also D&T Tree Service to consider. Vermont had trees, of course, but with Lane turning so much of his attention to the brewery, Case relocating would probably be the end of the company their fathers had started when they were younger than Case and Lane were now.

He couldn't leave Stonefield. Not right now, anyway. And probably not for a long time.

I can't.

He waited. The whiteboard disappeared and he waited again, for what felt like half a lifetime, but it wasn't coming back. Then her room went dark.

It was over.

Swallowing hard against the lump in his throat, he closed his curtains and walked out of his bedroom. Boomer followed, his mood subdued as he glanced repeatedly at his person for reassurance everything was okay.

Everything was definitely not okay.

With no way to fill the empty void that his life suddenly was, he sank onto the couch and turned on the television. Usually Boomer would flop on the floor or lay on the other end of the couch with his head up on the throw pillow as if he were any other guy watching TV, but he knew his person needed a little extra love.

Case couldn't help smiling down at his dog when he sprawled on his back with his head on Case's lap, offering his belly to be rubbed. He obliged, rubbing

Boomer's belly with one hand while mindlessly surfing channels with the other.

"You're a good boy, Boomer," he said in a soft voice, because petting his dog *did* help a little. "We'll be okay. Eventually."

Chapter Eighteen

The word around town is that the grand open-ing of Sutton's Place Brewery & Tavern was a big success! Combine a casual and relaxed atmosphere with excellent beer, and it's sure to become a favorite gathering place for our town. And it's a good thing it's not far from the Stonefield House of Pizza because the food or-ders kept the S-HoP delivery team busy!
—Stonefield Gazette *Facebook Page*

It was a lot harder to say goodbye to her family than Gwen had anticipated. Usually she gave them each a quick hug, got in her car and drove away. Not this time.

It had started as soon as she appeared in the

kitchen that morning, with Jack and Eli trying to talk her out of leaving by telling her all the fun stuff they could do if she stayed. And some of it even sounded fun. In the past there had been dutiful hugs for their aunt, but she'd spent more time with them this summer than she ever had before, and they weren't happy to see her go.

But she needed to go. She *had* to finish her book. And then she'd have to start another. It was harder to do that here. And there was nothing more she could do in Stonefield. The brewery was open. She and Case were over. It was time to go home.

It took less time than she'd imagined to pack up her car, and even though she felt as if she was dragging her feet, it wasn't even noon when her family gathered in the driveway to see her off. Her mom had even called Laura to the thrift shop again, so she could be there to say goodbye.

She wasn't surprised her mom was weepy about her leaving, of course. And Mallory always hated it when Gwen left. What really surprised her, though, were the tears in Evie's eye, and the swell of emotion she felt as she wrapped her arms around her youngest sister.

"I liked working with you," Evie said into Gwen's hair, her voice choked with tears.

"I liked working with you, too." And she had. They'd felt like a team—the Sutton sisters—and she was going to miss that more than she would have guessed. "I'm going to come back more often."

"Promise?"

"I promise." She didn't tell Evie it might be a little while before that first visit, though, because her heart wasn't going to be able to take seeing Case anytime soon—not without breaking all over again.

Her mother had already hugged her a dozen times, but there was another, of course. More tears. There were no words, but they didn't need any. It was all there in the fierceness of her mother's embrace. Then it was Mallory's turn.

"Text me when you get there," her sister told her in what probably would have been a very effective stern mom voice if she wasn't trying so hard not to cry.

Then quick hugs from Jack and Eli—who would miss her but also had Lego sets to build—and she was free to go.

It's the right thing, she told herself firmly.

She opened her car door, but she had to look—just one more time. Case's house was quiet, but his truck was in the driveway. And, from her window, she'd seen Boomer out in the yard earlier, while she was doing a final sweep of her room to make sure she had everything. But right now it was so still across the street, she'd think nobody was home if not for his vehicle.

He wasn't going to come out and say goodbye. And she didn't have the strength it would take to walk across the street and knock on his door to say that word to him.

Then she looked up and saw the white poster board in his bedroom window.

We'll miss you.

"I have to go," she said, not meaning to say it out loud, but the murmurings from her family made it clear she had and that they thought she was talking to them, rather than to herself. Or maybe to Case. Both.

She wasn't sure how she managed to get out of the driveway and through town while crying, but as Stonefield faded in her rearview mirror, so did the tears. There was nothing but numbness left, an emptiness that consumed her as she drove as though on autopilot.

About an hour and a half later, when she was only a few miles from putting New Hampshire in her rearview mirror, she caught herself going under the speed limit. It was the third time so far, and it was clear her subconscious was trying to send her a message.

She didn't really want to go home to Vermont.

She should have been relieved to be leaving Stonefield. She was going back to the life she'd made for herself, and she'd be free to resume her routine and get some writing done. Finish her book. Catch up on business.

Instead, the closer she got to crossing over the Connecticut River, the worse she felt—like an empty shell that was fragile, but it wouldn't matter if she broke because there was nothing inside, anyway.

I can turn around.

Her hands trembled slightly on the wheel as she considered the words that blindsided her. She could simply find a place to turn around and drive back to Stonefield. She could make a life with Case. Be a part of the everyday lives of her mother and her sisters. She could be there for her nephews and not just be the video chat aunt. She'd be free to help out at Sutton's Place on a very part-time basis. But she'd be a part of it.

Mostly, though, it was Case. With each mile she put between them, it became harder and harder to imagine what the rest of her life would look like without him in it. She couldn't see herself alone in her house, sipping really good coffee with her notebook. She couldn't really see anything at all. Instead she felt it. Her life would be lonely. Empty. Hollow. Could she even write that way? Did she want to?

And how long would it be before she stopped wanting to talk to him or share something funny with him?

She already missed his laugh. The feel of his fingers sliding through hers to hold her hand. She missed everything about him. And Boomer, too. Would she ever again feel as content as she had when she leaned into Case's arm while they watched a movie with the dog's head heavy on her lap?

When she passed vast, colorful fields of chrysanthemums, she knew she was but a few moments from being back in Vermont, and it was suddenly hard to breathe. Her heart ached in her chest and it was hard to swallow past the lump in her throat.

What the hell was she doing?

Tears were threatening to blur her vision, so Gwen braked hard and turned into a dirt driveway. There weren't any other vehicles in sight, and she hoped the farm's owners wouldn't mind if she parked there for a few minutes so she could get some fresh air and maybe get control of her emotions before she drove off into a ditch.

Water had always calmed her so, after taking a moment to compose herself, she walked out onto the bridge. The river dividing the state she'd been born in from the state she'd chosen to call home was quiet today, and she made her way to about the halfway point. Imagining herself standing on the state line, she took out her phone and snapped a few photos so a woman standing on the side of the bridge wouldn't alarm any passing drivers, but mostly she just needed a clear moment to think.

She could have it all. Her family. The bar. Her career—even if she had to rent an office space with a door that locked and leave her phone in the car. And most importantly, she could have Case. He could be hers to love for the rest of her life.

All she had to do was turn her car around.

"I don't know what we're going to do when we get to Vermont," Case told Boomer, who was happily looking out the passenger side window. He didn't care where they were going or what Vermont was. Case had promised the dog they'd find Gwen, and he got to the ride in the truck. Boomer was happy.

Case had made it *maybe* twenty minutes. The sound of her car pulling out onto the street and accelerating away had echoed through his very soul, making it hard to breathe. He'd tried to distract himself by emptying the dishwasher with the radio too loud. He'd even tried sitting on the floor and rubbing Boomer's belly.

He'd made it twenty minutes at the most before he realized he couldn't let her go this way. It couldn't be over.

But he had no idea how he was actually going to find her. She had a post office box, so he couldn't plug her address into his GPS. And he'd been in such a rush to go after her, he hadn't thought to ask Ellen or Mallory for her address. He could call one of them from the road, but he wanted to leave that as a very last resort just in case this mad dash wasn't enough and they really were over. It would be crushing enough without the Sutton women knowing about it.

He had a rough idea of where she lived—he knew the name of the town and that she lived on the outskirts of it—but short of going door-to-door, he wasn't sure how he was going to find her when he got there. His best chance of avoiding somebody calling the police on him was to catch her before she turned off the primary route, but he'd had to stop for gas. Now he was trying to find a balance between going fast enough to catch her without being reckless, but he didn't know the winding road at all.

He was almost to the bridge over the Connecticut when he spotted her car parked at what looked like the end of a dirt driveway for a farm. Putting his right arm across Boomer, he braked and took the unexpected left turn.

"Stay here for a minute, buddy," he told Boomer, who'd had a pee stop not too many miles ago and was content to curl up on the seat.

Leaving the truck running so Boomer wouldn't get hot and could listen to the radio, he got out and scanned the area.

His breath caught in his throat when he saw her, standing on the bridge and looking out over the river. He started toward her, not taking his eyes off of her as she took a photo. Then her shoulders lifted as though she'd taken a very deep breath and she put her phone in her pocket.

When she turned, presumably to walk back to her car, she saw him before she'd even taken the first step and froze.

He was just going to say it, he thought as he kept walking toward her. He was going to lay it all out there—everything he felt and wanted for their future—and no matter what happened after that, at least he would have tried.

There were tears in her eyes when he reached her, and he wanted to wipe them away, but he was afraid if he touched her first, he wouldn't get all the words out.

"I'll go with you." He realized he'd jumped right over some important stuff to say, so after taking a deep breath, started over. "I love you, Gwen. I love you and I want to spend the rest of my life with you, and if that means spending the rest of my life in Vermont, then I'm ready. The maple syrup isn't quite as good as ours, but other than that, it shouldn't be too hard an adjustment. We'll hire on a foreman for the tree service, and I can do administrative stuff from Vermont until we make a decision on what we want to do about it. And Boomer's on board with it."

Even though a tear had spilled over onto her cheek, she smiled. "He is, huh? Did he wag his tail extra hard?"

"Actually he was pretty mopey and when I asked if he wanted to go see you, he perked up and sprinted to the truck."

"Sprinted, huh?"

"Okay, it was more of an enthusiastic lope, but for Boomer, it was practically a sprint." He wiped the tear from her cheek with the pad of his thumb. "We both want to be wherever you are, no matter where that is."

"Do you know why I was standing on this bridge?"

The question confused him for a second. "I thought maybe you were stretching your legs. I saw you taking a picture. And I was happy you stopped, to be honest, because I didn't think you had that much of a head start and I was trying to catch you because I don't actually know where your house is.

You might want to read up on these things we have called speed limits, by the way."

She laughed, and then she reached out and took his hand, threading her fingers through his. "I was giving myself permission to turn around."

He started to open his mouth, but he was terrified suddenly that he was misunderstanding her. Maybe she'd given herself permission to walk back to her car and finish driving home. Or maybe she'd wanted to turn around to stop at some shop she'd talked herself out of stopping at. If she *didn't* mean that she was going to turn around and return to him, he wasn't sure he could stand it.

"As I got closer and closer to this bridge—to crossing over into Vermont—I found myself driving slower and slower."

"That doesn't make me feel any better about not catching up with you sooner," he said, because he needed to hear her laugh again. "Why were you turning around?"

"I was turning around because I'm in love with you, Case, and when I strip everything else away— my family and the annoying people in that town and the image of this life I'd built for myself—all I want is you. All I really need in this life is to be with you."

It was starting to sink in that Gwen had been coming back to him, and he wondered if she could feel his hand shaking. "I'm willing to move to Vermont if that's what you want. I meant that."

She looked over the river and exhaled slowly before smiling up at him. "It means everything to me that you'll do that."

"I can be packed up by the end of the week." Selling the house would take longer, but Ellen and Lane could help with that, and it wasn't as if he'd be in Alaska.

"There were a couple more light bulb moments while I was walking around," she said. "Obviously being in love with you was the high-wattage one, but I also like how close I am with my family again. And I like being a part of something that honors my dad, but even more, that we all built together. But mostly there's you. I love the *you* that you are now and taking you away from Stonefield would change you."

"Moving back to Stonefield changes *you*."

"But a good change." She shifted closer to him, and he had to remind himself that—standing on the side of the bridge as they were—that they were in a very public place. "I thought I was happy, but being with you and with my family is the life I want."

"Be my wife," he said, pulling her close. "I love you, and I want to spend the rest of my life making you happy. So, Gwen Sutton…will you marry me?"

"Yes," she whispered, and suddenly he was kissing her and she wrapped her arms around his neck. He never wanted to let her go again.

Then a car horn honked at them and they jerked apart in surprise. Laughing, he slid his fingers through hers and they walked hand in hand back to the New Hampshire side of the river. When they reached the truck, Case opened the door and told Boomer he could get out.

He went immediately to Gwen, his tail almost a blur as he threw his whole body weight against her legs so she could give him a good rubbing in greeting.

"He missed you," Case said. "We both did."

She laughed, trying to keep her balance as Boomer insisted on more back rubbing. "I wasn't gone that long."

"It was too long."

"Who's a good boy?" she crooned to the dog, and Boomer just wagged his entire butt because he knew, of course, that *he* was the good boy. "Let's go home."

Epilogue

Six months later

"We are *not* getting karaoke."

"Mallory, listen to me, though." Evie said, her voice raised to be heard over the laughter of the guys at the big table. "When people drink, they want to sing."

"Because drunk people think they *can* sing, and they are wrong. So very, *very* wrong. Gwen, back me up here."

Gwen laughed and shook her head. "I don't know what the right answer is. Yes, drunk people want to sing and karaoke is popular, but no, I don't want to hear these people singing karaoke."

Evie held up her hands. "There's no place to do karaoke in Stonefield, though."

"For good reason," Mallory insisted.

"You want to sing a sexy duet with me?" Case whispered in Gwen's ear, and she leaned back against him as his arms wrapped around her. Someday she hoped the tavern could afford proper barstools with backs, but Case's chest was a very nice substitute.

She turned her head so she could keep her voice low. "You know I can't sing, right?"

"Neither can I. When I said sexy duet, I meant for us. I think everybody else would want to cover their ears."

"Or drink faster, to drown out the pain." She laughed. "Solid marketing plan, though."

"We'll be opening soon," Ellen said, "and I'm going to take the boys to the movies tonight, but I wanted to say something before I go because it's our six-month anniversary."

"Tissues," Gwen whispered, and wasn't surprised when Case pressed a pocket pack of them into her hand. The man was really getting the hang of the Sutton women.

"David would be so proud of this place—and all of you." Ellen struggled to get the last few words out, so she paused and Gwen watched her struggle to fight back the tears. Nobody spoke because it was obvious Ellen had more to say, and eventually she was able to continue. "He'd be especially proud of his girls, because you all came together like this. You put aside your differences and made sacrifices to be by my side, and you not only helped make your father's dream come true but you gave me back a sense of stability, which I'd been missing since he went and died on me. Most of all, you brought me joy and helped heal my heart. To David."

When she lifted her glass, they all echoed her toast and it took some shifting around, but they all clinked glasses. "To Dad."

"And no more tears," she said. "We're celebrating."

"We have something else to celebrate, too," Case said, and Gwen groaned when her mother's face lit up, along with her sisters' and they all gasped. "No! No, not that. We're not pregnant. Yet. Crap, you tell them, Gwen."

She laughed. "I feel like the fact I'm finally finished with edits on my book and my editor loves the idea for my next one is a little anticlimactic if you're expecting a baby."

But her family cheered and embraced her as if she'd just given them the best news ever, and she appreciated that. She also appreciated the office Case had made for her out of one of the spare bedrooms. What would happen when they started filling those bedrooms with children, she wasn't sure, but they'd figure it out.

Together.

"Do you know what one of my favorite things about this bar is?" He was whispering in her ear again.

She sat up straight and turned on the stool so she was facing him Her family had scattered to start getting ready to open the doors, so she didn't bother whispering. "You've mentioned several times that you like when I'm trying to reach the glasses on the top shelf because it makes my boobs and my butt look great."

He nodded, giving her a grin. "There is that, though they always look great. Reaching for a glass just displays them a little extra. But another of my favorite things is that we live across the street."

Gwen laughed, nudging him with her shoulder. "You can have that extra beer and not worry about getting home. Maybe we should petition the town to put a crosswalk in for you."

Chuckling, he leaned in so he could press a kiss to the side of her neck. "Living across the street means you and I can sneak away for a few minutes here and there and nobody will notice."

His voice was low and rough, so close to her ear, and she shivered. "I'm not working tonight, so let's leave before they unlock the doors. They'll never notice."

"I've heard you're not very good at sneaking across the street, so we might as well say good-night."

She hooked her finger in the neck of his T-shirt and pulled him closer. "That'll be at least five minutes longer here. And that's only if we get out before they open."

Taking her hand, Case tugged her off the stool and they sprinted for the door, though she didn't make it all the way out before she started laughing. And she heard Mallory laughing, too, so she knew they hadn't done a very good job of sneaking.

Boomer must have been watching for them, because by the time they crossed the street, he was in the yard. They greeted him with pats and ear scratches, and then he walked between them toward the house while they held hands above him.

A car driving past beeped its horn and they both raised a hand in greeting without looking. As they climbed the steps of the front porch, Gwen realized it didn't matter who it was. The person behind the wheel was a friend, and in Stonefield you waved to everybody.

And when Case closed their front door and then pressed her up against it for a kiss that took her breath away, she felt the contentment all the way to her toes.

Home, she thought. It was definitely where the heart was.

We've received word from an observant reader this morning that a camper has appeared in the yard beside Sutton's Place Brewery & Tavern, which just celebrated six months of being our favorite hangout. Is somebody planning a vacation? Has a sibling squabble led to temporary exile from the house? Or perhaps the

Sutton family has a guest visiting from out of town and there's no more room at the (former) inn. Only time (and the Gazette!*) will tell!*
    —Stonefield Gazette *Facebook Page*

* * * * *